Mister Gum

or:

The Possibly Phoney Profundity of Puerility

by

Mr Gum

but

falsely attributed to

Rhys Hughes

"E by Gum!"

Cover art:
Water by Guiseppe Arcimboldo., 1563-4 (front).
Summer by Guiseppe Arcimboldo., 1563 (back).

This expanded second edition of *Mister Gum* includes an extra chapter, a new poem, a foreword by Joel Lane and an afterword by the author. Sections of this novel were previously published as a novella in *Polluto*.

Published in the United Kingdom by
Dog Horn Publishing
45 Monk Ings
Birstall
Batley
WF17 9HU

doghornpublishing.com
editor@doghornpublishing.com

A CIP record for this novel exists with the British Library.

This rude book is dedicated to:

Brian Willis, Hannah Lawson and **Huw Rees**

*because they have
suitably filthy
minds*

"The moon was emerging from behind the clouds, but it was not the moon, but a bum, a great bum spreading itself over the top of the trees. A childish bum over the world. Bum and nothing but bum. Behind me they were all wallowing in the *mêlée*, and in front of me was this great bum. The trees trembled in the breeze. And this great bum."

Witold Gombrowicz, *Ferdydurke*, 1937

Foreword: The Full Balzac

YOU ARE ABOUT to read the second edition of *Mister Gum* by Rhys Hughes. Having read the first edition, I recommend this book to you. And not only because it may have a better typeface this time round.

You may wonder: why have I been asked to write this introduction? I'm not a humorist, as those who know me will readily attest. Nor am I a noted Hughes enthusiast, though a few of his short stories have delighted me — most notably 'Lunarhampton' (a satirical portrait of Birmingham) and 'The Jam of Hypnos' (a lyrical dream narrative). But in general I'm the kind of writer (mostly grim and downbeat) whom Rhys sends up without mercy.

But I am inordinately fond of puns. My enthusiasm for wordplay began in childhood with the Puffin Club journal *Puffin Post*, edited by Puffin Books' founder Kaye Webb. One of their competitions involved drawing and naming new kinds of teapot, and the winners included a picture of a badly cracked teapot with the caption 'Porcelain teapot'.

My father was an influence too. He used to tell elaborate shaggy-dog stories that ended in puns on proverbs or quotations — years later, I realised they were modelled on the *My Word* radio monologues. He kept up the habit in later years — for example, once remarking to me that whereas the most original French writers were radical, the most original English writers were fairly right-wing. As I pondered this generalisation, he added, "So we lose the Bataille but win the Waugh."

For me, *Mister Gum* evokes the lost heroes of radio comedy: the punning anecdotes of Frank Muir, the surreal episodes of Spike Milligan, the audacious double entendres of *Round the Horne*. It would be impossible to film, but it could (and should) be recorded with sound effects. And bad music.

This book is so rich in fun it has transferred half of its jokes to Monaco to avoid paying tax on them. There's some well-deserved mockery of the prescriptive clichés of creative writing classes. There's a picaresque adventure involving the robbery of a sperm bank by two desperados wearing drawn-on stocking masks. There are strange one-liners like, "I hope they lock you up in a prison ship and throw away the quay." And much more besides.

One unifying theme runs (or rather drips) through the book: the power of sperm as a psychic and cultural symbol. But it's not a symbol of potency or fertility, rather of the narcissistic hunger of the male ego. There's no fertilisation and precious little intercourse in the world of *Mister Gum*, only an eternity of rod-stroking and spontaneous emission. As we choke in the grip of a global recession driven by the bankers — the whole voracious *wunch* of them — it's a resonant image.

This edition of *Mister Gum* has an added bonus: a new poem at the end that finishes off the book in fine satirical style. The first edition had a rather peevish afterword that mocked the BBC's *Late Review*. After I remarked to Rhys that I felt it ended the book on a sour note, he decided (with no pressure) to change it. And I have the pleasure of having helped to make an enjoyable book even better.

This novel is daft, facetious and extremely rude. However, it is neither crass nor meaningless. It celebrates the verbal imagination while highlighting the sheer pointlessness of many things we take for granted. It challenges the normative assumptions about 'the reader' that choke imagination, and annihilates the pomposity that surrounds the concept of the 'surreal' in modern genre fandom. Not bad for a book of wank jokes.

Wordplay and profanity are held in low regard in our culture because, like the bass guitar, they are not used to their full potential. Correctly harnessed, like the bass in the 'drum and bass' musical genre, they are both evocative and subversive. The stories of Ambrose Bierce and Robert Bloch use wordplay as finely sharpened instruments of terror (and so, unexpectedly, does August Derleth's dark gem 'Mrs Manifold').

In the work of Harlan Ellison, Conrad Williams and others, profanity is an intelligent driving force behind the most disturbing of narratives.

In *Mister Gum* the rhythm section are in command of the stage, and all the jokes are on their side. I could say that Rhys Hughes is the Roni Size of speculative fiction, but the words 'Rhys' and 'Size' don't really go together. What cannot be denied is that he is a writer with an exceptionally well-developed sense of irony. Why that is the case need not concern you.

One final point is worth noting. Despite his breadth of reading, Hughes is not the kind of writer who praises 'literary' culture above all else. His conversation largely revolves around practical experience, and his admiration is focused on those who change the world around them through action. He does not consider writers a breed apart. And so, for all his love of arcane literary devices, it's not literary theory that breaks through unexpectedly in Hughes' stories: it's the world.

Hughes' restless wit and nervous energy spring from his appetite for life. He does not use fiction to withdraw from reality, but rather to engage with it in unexpected ways. And in this book, concerned as it is with the absurdity of masculine sexual icons, it is the body — distorted, falsified, abused, hidden, but still alive — that has the last laugh.

Joel Lane
October 2010

Contents:

The Creative Writing Tutor

Oh, Whistle While You Work,
and I'll Come to You, My Dwarf

"SHOW, DON'T TELL," said my Creative Writing tutor. He had given the same advice at least ten times in every class and one night I decided to discover why 'showing' was so important to him and 'telling' so distasteful. I stayed behind after the other students had left and I put the question to him.

"I'll give you an answer if you insist," he sighed, "but why do you always sit at the back of the room? I don't like it."

"Anyway," he continued before I could reply, "it's good technique to depict a scene directly rather than relating it. I mean, let the reader work out what is happening and how to feel about it. Don't write something like 'the ship was very unlucky and fated to smash against rocks.' No. It's much better to conjure up a sense of doom with little clues: perhaps the flaking paint on the hull, the rolling yellow fogs, the odd habits of the captain . . .

"Any Creative Writing tutor will tell you the same thing.

"But in fact I have an extra reason for preferring 'showing' to 'telling'. I had a friend once who vanished for a year. One day he turned up and gave me a dreadful account of what had happened to him. He knew nothing about good writing technique and told his whole story in the wrong way, with lots of 'telling' and almost no 'showing'. It instilled a mortal terror of 'telling' in me that has persisted ever since. That's why I'm so strict with my students on this point.

"What was his story, I can almost hear you ask?

"Well, it seems he got himself a job as a chaperone to a young lady. A distant cousin had a virginal daughter who had enrolled in university in a distant foreign city. This cousin asked my friend — let's call

10

him Mr Mug — to escort the daughter — who we can name Primula — safely all the way. By 'safely' I mean with her virginity intact and by 'all the way' I mean the opposite of what you're thinking!

"They boarded an unlucky ship that was fated to smash against rocks ... Mention the fogs, damn it! Flaking paint on the captain's beard ... The ship went down and they jumped overboard. They lost everything and their clothes were shredded on the jagged reef and they were both washed up completely naked on the beach. Mr Mug and Primula were the only survivors who lived!

"Yes, his sentence structure really was that bad ...

"One other item was washed up next to them, a curious whistle. To cut a long story short, as the cliché said to the actress, this whistle was an antique, a device fabricated by the Knights Templar in the Ages of the Middle, and it had been brought aboard by an evil scholar whose speciality was magic ... Mr Mug remembered a conversation on deck with the scholar that went something like this:

" 'Abysmal weather for travelling on the high seas, what?'

" 'Yes indeed, but I don't care because I have ownership of a whistle that makes bedsheets come alive if you blow it.'

" 'Bedsheets, you say?'

" 'Certainly and all other types of fabric too!'

"The bedsheets didn't really come alive, they were merely borrowed by a disembodied spirit to help give it form: the scholar was very insistent on that point. The blowing of the whistle called the spirit and the spirit clothed itself in whatever 'garment' was available, even dirty napkins if that's all there was[1]. But this was irrelevant to Mr Mug. He cared only that ownership of the whistle had now passed to him.

"He supported Primula and they limped together along the beach, shouting for help, but nobody came. The sun went down somewhere behind the fogs and it grew cold as well as dark. How to keep warm

---

[1] Consult any good volume of the complete short stories of M.R. James for further information about this whistle.

11

without clothes? No, what you are thinking is vile! He didn't lay a finger on her: she was related to him.

"Not to beat about the bush, as the overused phrase said to the bishop, they huddled chastely in a hollow in the dunes and Mr Mug wondered what might happen if he blew the whistle. There were no sheets or fabrics of any kind in the vicinity. Mr Mug had a half-baked notion that the disembodied spirit might bring its own bedsheet, that this entity might then be shaken out and cast into the chill wind and the leftover sheet used to cover Primula and he.

"Tricking a phantom is always a risky business!

"Half baked notions and icy temperatures are a bad combination. Mr Mug raised the whistle to his lips and exhaled air into it but no bed-sheets came. Instead, the disembodied spirit took shape in the only thing available that even remotely resembled a piece of fabric. It materialised in Primula's unbroken hymen!

"Yes, that's where it appeared. A little face with little eyes and nose and mouth, all puckered up from an intact maidenhead! Mr Mug recoiled at the sight, a sight staring him in the face, for the grimaces of this perverted imp had forced Primula to widen her legs as far as possible. The face mouthed a silent obscenity at Mr Mug and rolled its sightless eyes.

"Mr Mug shook an admonishing finger at it — at a non-stimulating distance — but the hymen rippled and pulsed mockingly.

"Like the membrane of a voodoo drum!

"What could Mr Mug do to silence and banish this horrid creature, this labial lamia, this vaginal vampire? The obvious solution was out of the question: one does not knowingly thrust one's member in a demon's face. Sure enough, Mr Mug cared not to sheathe his pork sword in the visage of a cunt fiend! Excuse the language: my friend's writing style was grossly immature. All the same he had a point. I wouldn't hump a pussy ghost!

"He had no choice but to endure its presence all night long. In the morning the shipwrecked pair rose awkwardly and continued walking

12

down the beach, Primula's gait very wide, Mr Mug's not quite so. Her hymen remained a face that demonstrated no inclination to go away. Further along the beach they spied a pile of clothes. Two bathers were splashing about in the surf: civilisation was near. Mr Mug and Primula stole the clothes and continued along the shore until they reached a port town, a tangle of narrow cobbled alleys, whitewashed houses, slave markets and brothels.

"Lacking money and style, what could Mr Mug do? Lacking a method of banishing the quim monster himself, what could he doubly do? To earn cash and rid himself of the hymen spirit at one and the same time, he sold poor Primula into prostitution.

"Now he had enough spare cash to return home. But he didn't go back immediately. He hung around the port town for a month, lodging in a reasonable hotel, unable to leave until he knew what had happened to Primula's possessed hymen. In the cheapest bars he heard no gossip, nothing to indicate that brothels were now a place to be feared. No tale emerged of the unknown man who had deflowered Primula, no anecdote about a genital genie.

"In a fury of curiosity Mr Mug disguised himself as one of those men who pay for sexual encounters and entered the brothel as a customer. In an ill-lit room he beheld Primula again, taking care she did not recognise him. He did nothing physical, for that would have been gross, but merely asked her to undress. He saw what he needed to see and departed in confusion.

"Her hymen and the demon that possessed it were both gone! But where? And this raised a bigger question: where does any hymen go when it is broken? When virginity is taken, where is it taken to? Mr Mug didn't know and nor do I.

"He returned home and lived a normal life. But that question haunted him forever more. Nor could he shake away from his mind the image of that little being with its little face and little expressions. Better if the creature had been enormous, appearing in the sail of an old-time ship, for example. Anything other than that hideous dwarf!

13

"And so Mr Mug's story comes to an end. But it isn't really his story. So utterly dismal was his writing technique that he resorted to concealing his identity with a simple trick: reversing the letters of his surname!

"That's right, there is no 'Mr Mug'. There is only 'Mr Gum' and that's me! Mr Gum the Creative Writing tutor. The story I have just told actually happened to me, not to him, because there is no 'him', he's just an invention. Some people claim that teaching Creative Writing isn't real work. But it is!

"So there you have it. 'Show, don't tell' has been my motto ever since. But I still want to know why you always sit at the back of the class?"

He squinted at me through his spectacles and I replied, "To be honest, I'm not sitting at the back, but at the front, almost under your nose. These tables and chairs that separate us are tiny models arranged to confuse your sense of perspective."

"So they are!" he roared, "and touching them, I realise they are made from loose flaps of skin. Exactly the flaps of skin that might be found in a brothel where virgins work!"

I grinned. "So they do! And now I'll tell you where hymens go when they are broken. Some just lie around on the floor, waiting to be collected. Others gather themselves up and go wandering until they find the men who originally whistled for them. But now it's time for *me* to ask *you* a question: doesn't it strike you as odd that a hymen can be male?"

14

Boo to a Goose

"**R**ULES ARE MADE to be broken," said the Creative Writing tutor, "but only if you are a slimy liar or insignificant worm.

"I'm not exaggerating. The best writers don't break rules . . .

"Don't argue with me, I know what I'm talking about, I'm Mr Gum the Creative Writing tutor, I get paid to do this job, and I declare that the rules of good writing are immutable.

"In other words they never change and they can't decay.

"A clumsy oaf might be able to snap parts of them off, but those parts will always remain strong and viable.

"Are you listening? I guess you think my voice is a bit odd, that my tongue isn't like a normal man's tongue. If you think that, you'd be right. My tongue is indeed very strange.

"Anyway, of all the rules that get broken but shouldn't, there are three more important than the others. Let me explain what they are. Only write what you know. That's the first.

"*Only write what you know.* I've repeated that rule in italics to make sure there's no misunderstanding.

"For example, I once wrote a short story about prog rock musicians. I bet you think that owning several hundred prog rock albums and knowing the names of the guitarists from Yes and Genesis and maybe even playing in a prog rock band qualifies a writer to write about prog rock. Sadly the case is not that. It takes more.

"If you've never cracked nuts with a prog rock musician, or impaled cubes of cheese and pineapple on little sticks with one, then you have no right to write a prog rock story. None.

"The real world is the real place to learn real things . . .

15

"In the case of prog rock, preparing savoury snacks is the real way to immerse yourself for real in the real prog rock scene, because that's what prog rock musicians do when they aren't doing prog rock, or so I've been told, by a real teller in my real ear.

"A good writer uses the world for inspiration, the real world, not his or her imagination. And the real world is full of real people. Real people do real things. Some of those real people are prog rock musicians, as I've already strongly hinted, but many others are homosexuals and they have real homosexual sex. Yes they do.

"Hard to believe, but that doesn't mean it's not true. And in fact it *is* true. Homosexuals. Out there.

"Let me tell you a tale about myself, but in fact it's not about myself but about Mr Mgu, a man identical in every way to me except that he had lots of homosexual sex when I didn't.

"How much is 'lots', I hear you ask? Tons, I reply!

"Tons of juicy homosexual sex!

"But the word 'homosexual' is offensive to most modern liberals, so I intend to say 'gay' from now on.

"Thoughtful, aren't I? Indeed I am! But I'm not gay. Never oiled a boy in my life. Not once. Not last month.

"Warm slippery golden oil over his buttocks. Nope.

"Nor did a boy or any man variant oil my own buttocks. Shaft of cock proud in the dim smoky light . . .

"Tangents are acceptable in good writing, the fine writing of the best writers, the writing found in the unpublished novels of Mr Mgu. So don't berate me when I say things like: moist rough tongue flicking throbbing purple man meat to spurting joy! That's a tangent. Sucking rigid cock, hot in cheek pouch, licking veined length, chewing lightly, spurt in face! Yes, a tangent. Not gay talk. Cock.

"Where was I? Ah yes, writing what I know — or rather what Mr Mgu knew — when he decided to write what he knew . . . A new novel about the real world, the world I've already described, full of real stiff cocks really being sucked to real satisfaction. Imperative to know it!

16

Yes, to know hot gay sex for real in the real world. Real cock, real suck, real hard. Come in my mouth but save some for my face.

"Now then, Mr Mgu didn't know the first thing about cock, so he had to learn from scratch, but he was dedicated and he went in search of it. He knew he'd recognise it for what it was when he found it. Thrusting pelvis, taut buttocks, peachy pork pillar . . .

"This is all getting confused. I think I might have given you the wrong impression. Mr Mgu didn't want to have the cock he found — if find one he ever did — stuffed in his mouth with the creamy goodness spraying the back of his throat . . . No he wanted to force his *own* cock into a little eager mouth, between lips compressed just enough, work it more roughly, push to the back of the throat, harder.

"I love fucking boys. I want to throat fuck boys.

"That was Mr Mgu speaking, not me. I can't imagine anything worse than throat fucking a boy, yanking his head more roughly onto the hilt of my enormous tool with masterful strong hands while his eyes widen in surprise and he feels a little panic and sucks harder to get the job done so I won't keep forcing him down, obstructing his narrow windpipe with my swollen conic section, pushing into his throat, brutally, not caring about his discomfort, caring only to shoot my load, suffocating him, boneless joy column grating against teeth.

"I like to kiss my own sperm from bruised lips straight after . . . Or so claimed Mr Mgu when I asked him about it . . . And I believe him. Don't you? Well you should. Salty.

"Anyway, Mr Mgu happened to be in Madrid. Men often happen to be in places. All the time in fact. Some place or other. Madrid has a vibrant gay quarter called Chueca where cocks are frequently sucked, some say sucked without cessation, but I've already warned you about hyperbole so let's just say: many hot cocks, much sucked.

"Buggery also. Sphincter muscle pulsing rhythmically, explosion deep in lower bowel, prostrate milk a-trickle.

"Mr Mgu walked into a gay club for research purposes.

17

"The name of the club was *To Boldly Go*. That's a split infinitive, very bad — the split in the infinitive I mean, not the alluring split between the bum cheeks of smooth firm boys.

"Poor grammar notwithstanding, in he went.

"He sat on a stool at the bar and ordered tea and then he also ordered a smooth firm boy but the barman just looked at him in confusion and so did the other customers. '¿Que?' they kept repeating, over and over, and the inverted question mark at the beginning of that word irked Mr Mgu's best unwaxy ear like a rusty tuna hook.

"Unwashed cocks smell like tuna also, Mr Mgu later revealed. To me. When I asked him to reveal things . . .

"He raised his voice a few decibels. 'Smooth firm boy!' cried he with forceful manly decisiveness, but still those Spaniards didn't understand, and then he realised that foreigners who don't speak English would never know what a smooth firm boy was unless he showed one to them, and to do that he had to ask for one first. So he was stuck in a loop of negative comprehension. Cocks uncurling.

"His only hope was to learn Spanish, but he was too impatient to stuff his wedge up a rectum, or down a throat, for that. The idea that a wedge might be stuffed *down* a rectum or *up* a throat simply never occurred to him. And why should it? Was Mr Mgu a surrealist? He was not. Was he a great writer? Verily he was!

"But mostly unpublished. Unfair!

"Luckily for Mr Mgu, or unluckily if you jump to the end of my story, which you can't because you're listening to it, not reading it, in walked a man who spoke English as well as foreign. He saw the cup of tea in Mr Mgu's hand, a hand containing five fingers easily able to wank a boy to submission, and he nodded wisely.

"Then he said, 'English are you, buster?'

"To which Mr Mgu replied, "Absolutely and rightly so.'

"The newcomer asked, 'What's your desire, chum?'

"Mr Mgu answered, 'Smooth firm boy.'

"The newcomer grinned. 'How do you want him?'

18

"Mr Mgu considered the matter. 'Chained to the bed.'

"The newcomer took Mr Mgu by the hand and led him to the rear of the club, through a little door, down a long corridor that twisted like a boy's intestine, illuminated by spherical white lamps that resembled big globs of spunk on the walls, and towards a curtain. 'Step through here, old son,' sayeth the newcomer, 'and you'll get your desire right enough. Cock at the ready, huh? ¡Vamos!'

"Mr Mgu was utterly without suspicion, so he stepped through the curtain. Suddenly it was a dark and stormy night! No it wasn't. On the contrary he was sliding down a greased chute under the club with that awful name, *To Boldly Go*, faster and faster, his velocity increasing and his acceleration also. Cock. Suck.

"The newcomer had tricked him into falling through a trapdoor. The chute sped him onwards. Where would it end? It kept going. Bloody hell, it was a long chute. No friction, thankfully!

"Thankfully or *wankfully*? A question not yet resolved!

"Soon Mr Mgu was travelling at 100 kph. His entire journey lasted six hours. Who's a clever smarty-pants in my class who can calculate where he ended up? That's right. In the sea!

"The chute ejaculated him into the briny ocean . . .

"A bad swimmer was he, and drowned was sure to be his obituary's verdict, but then he noticed something floating nearby. He didn't have the strength or skill to make for the coast but he reckoned he could reach this orange ball thing. And so he did.

"It was a smooth firm buoy. Chained to the bed — the seabed!

"Listen to me, my students, for I care deeply about you and I want you to write good works, good real works with good real words, so heed this advice, for 'tis most pertinent . . . NEVER resort to bad puns in a piece of prose. Never, never, never, never, never!

"Why should a dog, a horse, a rat, have life and my flaccid cock none? That's Mr Mgu speaking again.

"He can't get it up these days, after his experiences.

19

"Never using puns is the second most important rule of all the rules of writing that shouldn't get broken.

"Only write what you know is the first. Remember?

"Anyway, Mr Mgu reached the smooth firm buoy safely and clung he there for dear — and budget — life. He reasoned that a ship might pass and rescue him, perhaps before nightfall.

"His reasoning was sound. A ship did approach.

"But it was very old fashioned, with sails and cannons and stuff like that, and the captain who looked over the side and called to Mr Mgu wore a bicorn hat and an eyepatch.

"He cast a rope ladder at the excellent author and Mr Mgu climbed to safety. 'Horatio Nelson, I presume?' asked he.

"The captain clearly never attended one of my creative writing courses because he replied, '*Fellatio* Nelson, dear boy.'

"Mr Mgu winced. 'Fucking awful pun . . . You blighter!'

"Fellatio Nelson winked. 'Get down on your knees, laddie me boy, for I'm a paedophileophile, don't you know.'

"Mr Mgu was outraged. 'That's disgusting! A paedophile, you say?'

"Fellatio Nelson shook his head slowly. 'You aren't listening, are you? I didn't say 'paedophile', I said *paedophileophile*. Underage boys and girls do nothing for me, but I'm massively aroused by the thought of forcing a paedophile to suck me off.'

"Mr Mgu stamped his foot. 'In that case, look elsewhere, for I'm not a paedophile, I'm a brilliant writer.'

"Fellatio Nelson sneered. 'Of course you're a paedophile . . . You asked for a smooth firm boy, did you not? A *boy*, not a man! Now get down on your knees and part those lips of yours . . . '

"Mr Mgu refused. He did the exact opposite of what was demanded of him, turning his back to Fellatio Nelson, pulling off his trousers and then bending over the rail of the ship.

"In this position he thought cocksucking was out of the question, but Fellatio Nelson merely guffawed and pulled down his own trousers. His member was astounding, as long as a hosepipe and just as green,

20

and with a deft motion he thrust it up Mr Mgu's vulnerably exposed anus. Into his bowels went this odd cock, swerving around the bends of his guts, blindly flapping in the stomach, then up into the slick throat and finally out of the mouth, where it rested on Mr Mgu's tongue.

"Backwards fellatio! Cocksucking from within!

"Mr Mgu yelled, 'You'll have to remove that monstrous sausage at some point and that's when I'll escape.'

"Fellatio Nelson responded, 'I'm going nowhere.'

"Mr Mgu growled, 'In that case, you'll decay while fixed to my rump. Then I'll be free anyway!'

"Fellatio Nelson hissed, 'Not so! I'm immutable, like the rules of good writing, and I can never change or decay. You might be able to snap parts of me off, but those parts will remain viable and strong.'

"Mr Mgu reacted to this clue. He wriggled until he heard a crack, then he jumped overboard. Fellatio Nelson howled in pain. His cock was still lodged in the author's body, running the entire length of his alimentary canal like an entrepreneurial tapeworm, and he never managed to remove it ever since. Somehow he survived the sea and was washed ashore but I don't remember how that happened.

"Now Mr Mgu has two tongues and can speak with both of them, but if he speaks too much with the upper one he comes. I've almost said too much during this lesson and soon I'll spray the nearest of you with pearly man dew, for Mr Mgu is actually me, Mr Gum the Creative Writing tutor! But before I shoot my load over your eager studious faces, like a sort of bukkake man cow, allow me to reveal the third and possibly worst of all the rules that should never be broken if you want to write a decent story and get published by publishers.

"This is the third rule — avoid using titles that are totally unconnected to the story. Now I'm about to come.

"Yes, yes, oh yes. Thanks. Goodnight."

Whaling Well

"**E**VERY STUDENT IN this room," declared the Creative Writing tutor, "is a fool — present company excepted!

"Did you notice what I just did?" he continued. "That's right, I constructed a self-negating sentence. Was it clever of me?

"No!" he thundered, before anyone could answer. "It was glib and pompous — like prog rock music. Prog rock pretends to be stupendous and cerebral but isn't, just like certain kinds of flashy writing, the kind that revels in silly anachronisms and sentence inversion doth employ.

"You can be certain I never resort to such tricks in my own fiction — work brutally shorn of metaphors, similes, pataphors, metafictional japes and all other ornamental doodles on the marvellously smooth marble walls of the imaginary opera house that is my mind. No cherubs for me, buster!

"How is it possible for a prose style to be so manly and clear?

"It's simply the result of my astounding self discipline. A billion times have I forced myself to refrain from using hyperbole.

"I don't even have time for tm-bloody-esis[2]. But perhaps we're getting too technical for this class of beginners. Or perhaps I should say 'beginner', for there appears only to be a single student in my class to-night."

And he frowned at the man who sat hunched over a little desk nearest the window, a position from which the sea was visible, already slate grey in reality but doubly greyed by the grimy glass until it seemed a cleaner black, like the thick juice of lost submarines caught and squeezed by the giant hands of the impossible traffic policemen who direct the movements of gloopy monsters at the bottom of the ocean,

---

[2] Nobody else has the time either. It's surprising tmesis still exists. *C'est-la*-fucking-*vie*.

nightmarish beasts with eyes and opinions in unexpected places. This sentence contains some other nonsense in keeping with the pointless whimsicality of the general paragraph. But this next sentence doesn't. That's called versatility.

"What did you say your name was?" the tutor demanded.

"I prefer to be known as The Postmodern Mariner," came the reply, "and even though I feel the pseudonym is slightly ridiculous, because it seems to promise more than I can deliver — constant blending of allusions from all periods of human culture — it's how my readers know me. That's called consistency."

"Your *readers*?" came a gasp of shock. "You are a *published* writer?"

"I have a blog," responded The Postmodern Mariner.

"Ah, only a blog. So there's no need for me to tie a knot of jealousy and envy in my stomach or endure that soul-jarring sensation when one feels they are slipping down an incline towards a pit of non-achievement and wasted life. Good, I am cheered by your confession. After all, who's the one teaching this class, me or you? Me, of course, I'm the expert, Mr Gum, the Creative Writing tutor!"

"I report on the mysteries of the ocean deeps only . . . "

"Stranger things always happen at sea, as the saying goes, a maxim that fills me with horrified curiosity when I consider the strange things that have happened on land — the Immaculate Conception, for instance. Logically, if a woman can get pregnant without having sex on land, she is able to do something even more extreme on a boat. Harpoon whales with her clitoris, perhaps?"

"I have never encountered such a case," stated The Postmodern Mariner, "and I doubt sufficient elongation and firmness of the gland in question could ever be attained for the operation you specify. Even the paranoid cetacean, Moby K Dick, can't be speared that way and he's made mostly of pink light."

"You mean that somebody has tried?" muttered Mr Gum, turning pale.

"I hear rumours, whisperings, hints . . . I want to write these down properly in a sober manner, to produce a piece akin to a cool headed academic report, and I've enrolled on this course entirely for that reason."

Mr Gum paced back and forth for a whole minute, then he paced forth and back for a second — a second minute, not a single second — and then back and back for a third, and finally forth and forth for a fourth.

"You were very wise to do so," he declared. "I plan to tell you a story to enlighten you about a topic you've raised, a tale about a fellow called Mr Umg, but before I do that I'm going to instruct you in one of the most important rules of the art of creative writing, but before I do *that* I want you to demonstrate your own writing style, so I can judge whether you are untrainable or not. It might be that you are already too far gone, as often happens with writers of blogs."

"I have to write a story now?" The Postmodern Mariner asked.

"Just speak it to me . . . As you are only a fictional character, everything you say will appear in words anyway, words written by the real author of this story — that chap out there. I know that seems like a cheap metafictional ruse, and earlier I said I had no time for metafictional japes, but we're talking about you, not me, and you did say your name was The *Postmodern* Mariner, did you not?

"As much as I disapprove of that movement," continued Mr Gum, "it does make life easier for us in such situations. When we speak, our author is forced to take dictation. We never need to hold a pen in our lives! No hand cramps for us, apart from those that come from excessive wanking. Having said that, I don't spank the monkey like normal men, I prefer to hump my pillow or cut a hole in a melon — actually a kiwi shaved to resemble a melon — or put my dangly between two firm conference pears and give a pearl necklace to the rest of the fruitbowl.

"You can also find pearls under the sea," he added thoughtfully.

24

The Postmodern Mariner nodded his agreement. He remembered the time a gigantic oyster had given *him* a pearl necklace, very gently because it had been his first time, and this memory suggested something else, for oysters are not so different from clams, so he decided to fulfil his obligation to Mr Gum by relating the tale of the longest lived clam in the world. And this is how he did that:

"Did you know that clams exhibit rings just like trees do?"

"No I didn't," said Mr Gum.

"Well they do," continued The Postmodern Mariner.

"I'm listening," prompted Mr Gum, "but before you proceed I want you to do a big favour for me. Kindly hold this bag."

"Like this?" asked The Postmodern Mariner.

"Indeed so. It contains two small coconuts. Now resume your blather!"

The Postmodern Mariner nodded. "For every year that passes, a clam adds a ring to its shell, and a decade ago a scientist from the University of Bangor — that's a town in Wales — on an expedition around the shores of Iceland dredged up a specimen with no less than 405 rings. Turns out this was the oldest animal ever discovered! The scientist became famous in a small way and was very happy, in fact he believed his contentment to be utterly complete, for he was in good health and reasonably wealthy and had a new young wife who was very attractive.

"Anyway, he decided to participate in a second expedition the following year to the same place, to see if an even older specimen might be found. Alas that he did! A storm came, the research vessel capsized and he sank into the sea. He should have realised the voyage was doomed from the beginning. There were many clues. The flaking paint on the hull, the rolling yellow fogs, the odd habits of the captain . . . Anyway, on the seabed, he was found by some curious clams who took him to their local university and counted his rings. Turned out he was the youngest scientist ever discovered! They only found one ring on him, his wedding ring!

25

"This story could have been more rude than that, but isn't."

The Postmodern Mariner puffed out his cheeks and added hopefully, "What do you think? Am I trainable or not?"

There was a long anguished pause.

"The important rule I want to impart to you," said Mr Gum very forcefully, "a rule so crucial to producing good creative writing that it ought to be engraved on the inner eyelids of every aspiring author, is this: the reader should always identify totally with the main character of your story.

"You dig that, baby? Total identification . . .

"I'm sorry to say that I couldn't identify with the main character in your story, I'm not even sure who *was* the main character, the scientist or the clam? So let me show you how it ought to be done.

"Are you ready, dude? Get set. Here we go . . .

"Did you ever meet a fellow called Fellatio Nelson? You didn't! Too bad. He sailed the oceans of the world in a sailing ship with sails. He had a notable cock, a powerful prehensile cock, a cock so long and flexible it could snake into the jungle from the shore and strangle strange snakes for sure! That cock doubtless could sneak into pockets and snatch wallets, or play fig tree wrap with elephant trunks — that reference requires some knowledge of the behaviour of trees — and it's possible it did both things, for I know my wallet went missing on more than one occasion because of cock. In Manchester. But to return to the point, he sailed around.

"Yep, all the watery places of this blue globe were his soft and salty garden and he liked to hoe and rake it for as long as that very dubious metaphor might last. Hunting whales was one of his passions, as well as raping paedophiles, and he always employed his cock as the fateful lance for both operations. Don't you feel his character developing with every subsequent sentence? That's the way to write, honey pie. Now then, sonny, listen up, because it turns out he himself was being hunted, by a man he did wrong to a long time before, a man called Mr Umg.

26

"Yes indeed. Mr Umg — no relation to Messrs Mug and Mgu, obviously, because the surnames are different — wanted revenge, and sweareth he to taketh it before the end of the financial year, and doughty in heart and buttock set he off on his quest to trim Sir Fellatio's wick, rightly good withal.

"Trouble was, no inkling had he of how to conduct such an operation. Then a stroke of luck . . . Word came to his ear, an ear shaped like a duchess's cunt, that a bloody huge sperm whale had been sighted inland, at the bottom of a deep well in a town in the land of Piedmont. The strings of the trap had been sharpened, the jaws of the snare knotted tightly, the turns of phrase mixed, and he — meaning Mr Umg — had expended no energy at all in the process. Hurrah!

"Are you following every detail closely, so far?"

"That I am," affirmed The Postmodern Mariner.

"Bueno. So let me continue," continued Mr Gum, "for the exciting bit is coming up about three sentences from now. Night. Sounds. Hammering. Mr Umg constructed a covering for the well, a lid in the shape of a pussy — not a cat, the other kind, modelled on one of his own ears. A right royal snatch.

"He knew that Fellatio Nelson would be irresistibly drawn to that particular well for three reasons: (1) the whale itself, (2) the *sperm* reference, and (3) the location of the well — Piedmont — sounded vaguely like the word paedophile, very vaguely indeed, but Fellatio was a very vague kind of guy, with a vague bicorne hat, vague eyepatch, vague *Kiss Me Hardy* badge on a vague blazer.

"True enough, after a few days of waiting, the target cock came into sight. Snaketh along the ground it did do! I forgot to mention that the well was truly massive, but my forgetfulness was deliberate, to add humanity to my story, because humans are mostly imperfect in the memory sphere. Savvy?

"The cock reared high — they sometimes do that — and plunged with incredible force into the opening of the well. But the well was a simulated quim, the cunny of a duchess, and Fellatio Nelson had vowed

27

only to penetrate paedophiles. This more conventional fuck was a vile travesty of sodomy to him, a violation of all his principles, and aghast was he to such an extent that he had a quick stroke — I don't mean he rubbed his hand on a passing crotch — and died of death.

"Mr Umg danced a victory dance like this. Watch my feet move, quicker than the eye! Gives me blisters, pus ripe, but anything for art's sake. Now that's over with, let me add that none of this happened, it's just a story, and stories are fictional, and the act of good Creative Writing lies in telling lies according to the rules, rules so strict they whip themselves in secret chateaus, and nothing else. To my best knowledge the whale wasn't harpooned before Fellatio keeled.

"What do you think? Before you answer let me give you a clue. The construction of that story was perfect. Total character identification was not only rendered possible but *easy* — or 'muy fácil' as they say in Spain.

"I once spent time in Madrid, by the way . . . But in fact it wasn't me but a chap named Mr Mgu . . . And yet I confess it was me.

"However, today we are talking about Mr Umg, not Mr Mgu, but if you really want to be awkward I'll announce there isn't a Mr Umg either, there's only ever me, just me, always me, Mr Gum, the Creative Writing tutor.

"So don't bother me with irrelevancies. Comprende?

"Now answer the goddam question. Did you identify or not? Well did ya, punk? And inci-pissing-dentally, tmesis or no tmesis, I actually like prog rock. You have a problem with that, heathen dog? I'm waiting."

The Postmodern Mariner was a little flustered. "I certainly identified with the main character of your tale," he responded, "but I'm sorry to say that the main character was the cock, not Mr Umg or Fellatio Nelson."

"You had total identification with the cock? Stand up!"

No sooner had The Postmodern Mariner climbed to his feet than Mr Gum ran at him and kicked the bag of small coconuts as hard as possible. There was a cracking noise and white liquid spurted. The coconuts were damaged as well. Hopping on his burst feet, slipping in his own cheesy pus, Mr Gum howled triumphantly and wagged his finger like a cock in the shape of a thumb.

"Now get out of my class and take this lesson with you. Right good and proper hath it been taught this darkling day. Fellatio Nelson could never have done the thing with his cock I've just described, because his cock is elsewhere, running the entire length of my alimentary canal in fact — but you don't need to know that, you pervert — and that's why fiction is called fiction, buddy boy, and not reportage! But when you identified totally with the main character, in essence you became his cock, if only temporarily, and by extension the bag of coconuts became his bollocks, and thus I have my revenge on that bastard! I am satisfied. All is over.

"You still here? Depart with the example of my incomparable methodology fresh in your second mind's eye, the one behind the mind's head connected to your first mind's eye. I always go an extra level deeper.

"Why the delay? This unbearable sinister delay! Begone!

"Are you leering at my ears?"

The Tenant of Arcimboldo Hall

"YOU CAN'T FENCE with a banana — unless your opponent is a famished chimp and the blade is poisoned," cried the Creative Writing tutor, "but that has nothing to do with anything and I resent you for making me say it.

"And bananas don't even have blades, they're a kind of fruit. I can tell this class has got off to a bad start. They sometimes do.

"So let's turn to more constructive matters . . . Punctuation!

"Punctuation is more important to the fledgling writer than bosoms to the titty wank enthusiast. I'm not one of those, by the way.

"But I bet *you* are, especially you and you and you down there.

"In which case, you have a teat — I mean treat — in store . . .

"Has anyone in this class ever heard of the very famous Lynne Truss[3]? She's truly a household name but some of you look as if you don't have homes. That makes it rather more tricky. No matter. I have a surprise for you, she's agreed to give a guest speech at our class tonight. Zounds and forsooth!

"In fact she'll be here in five minutes or so.

"Lynne Truss — I hardly need mention — is the goddess of punctuation. So revered is she in this area of expertise that not even Vatican officials dare use semi-colons without her permission. And speaking of the Vatican reminds me of a riddle, which I plan to set as homework: does the pope shit in the woods?

"More to the point, is a bear a catholic? Yes he is. Doubtless.

"Now then: I want you to prepare for Lynne Truss's visit by choosing your favourite punctuation mark and using it properly.

"Can, you? fucking; do: that!

---

[3] Literary editor of *The Listener* magazine (1986-90)

"I don't reckon you can, so it's up to you to prove me wrong, you callous creeps, to make me proud, but not stiff, not tonight anyway. One more thing: I don't want you goosing Lynne when she arrives.

"Partly because it won't be the real Lynne but an impostor!

"Yes, a man disguised as Lynne Truss, a devious man by the name of Mr Gmu, can you credit it? And to goose a man isn't always something to crow about, ducky. Anyone keeping an eye on the time? It flies, none can say whither! Show, don't tell, by the way, and write what you know — if you know anything, pigdogs that you are. As for myself, I don't know why Mr Gmu likes dressing up as Lynne Truss, so I can't write about it. But I do have a plan to get our revenge.

"My plan is this — we truss up Lynne Truss!

"The moment she/he steps through that door, up we jump, overpower her/him and bind his/her limbs with this rope I brought along, casually enough, then we force 'Ms' Truss to give her lecture anyway, for free!

"Christ on a beanpole, I think of everything, don't I just?

"Well she appears to be a bit late — those five minutes have gone fast, as minutes tend to do in stories, when the plot demands it — so I'll just pop into the corridor to see what might be keeping her. If you hear odd noises, maybe the sounds of a man changing into women's clothing, just ignore them.

"Stay out and don't follow me, you bloody voyeurs!

"Fine, I'm outside now and I still can't see any signs of our guest speaker, and this suspender belt is bloody killing me, but I'm Mr Gum, the Creative Writing tutor, and I'm a hardy soul, not given to complaining, unlike Mr Gmu, the transvestite grumbler, and I'm sure everything will work out.

"Ah! Here we are, my wig's in place, so here she is.

"Hello class, my name is Lynne Truss, I passed your tutor in the corridor, he seems like a wonderful chap, certainly worthy of getting his work published, so why hasn't it been, is there some sort of conspiracy going on, but anyway he said he had to go away on important business,

31

so he won't be coming back, you have just me for the whole night, my fee is 6000 euros, and I'll begin immediately by discussing the wonders of punctuation in all their shapes and sizes . . .

"What are you doing? Tying me up! Help, help: my virtue! Notice the colon, applied carefully even under shibari knots?

"Here's another: colon, in case you missed the first.

"Don't ever use 'em. Colons stink. Like shit. I'm Lynne Truss, yes I am, O yes, and if there's one thing I like more than having a hundred men use me for a communal titty wank, it's punctuation. Now then.

"When punctuation is misapplied, strange and dangerous things can happen. Few people in this world — I'm probably the only one — and maybe Martin Amis too — are competent enough to use punctuation absolutely correctly, heck I even understand the ramifications of the little known *Oxford comma*, which precedes the use of the word 'and' in lists, even when it seems such a comma is superfluous, as follows: bugger, sod, arse, tit, and wank. You dig that, chums?

"The Oxford comma is so called because in that town they like to punt and 'punt' is cockney rhyming slang for 'cunt', which is what the man who devised that comma was. Strange there should be so many cockneys in Oxford! Apples and pears, me ol' china! I will now demonstrate the amazing importance of the location of commas, in an ordered logical sequence, very clever of me, and please bear in mind that the comma is only one of many available punctuation marks!

"Consider this simple sentence — 'Sue me baby!'

"Depending on where the writer puts his commas, that sentence can mean many different things. Here are the variations:

"(1) Sue me, baby! (this means the speaker is daring his girlfriend to take him to court in an attempt to extract money),

"(2) Sue, me, baby! (a list of items),

"(3) Sue, me baby! (affirming colloquially his girlfriend is named Sue),

"(4) Sue me baby! (no comma: daring someone to take his baby to court),

32

"(5) Sue,,, me,,, baby! (the speaker is a retard).

"So a sentence containing only three words have can have five opposing meanings and all because of comma location! Are you astounded, you fuckwits? You should be. I'm Lynne Truss, do you like my tits?

"Now I'll relate to you a story to further illustrate the crucial significance of proper punctuation and how it can be a matter of life or death! Before I came here I debated with myself what tale to tell. An anecdote about Bram the Stoker or Bryan the Ferry or Diana the Rig? Not so! I even considered relating a yarn concerning Derrick the Haton, but in the end decided to tell one about a fellow by the name of Peter the Tenant. Once he was invited to a fancy dress party.

"Yes, a party where you have to dress in elaborations.

"But this party had a particular theme — all the guests had to wear costumes in the style of the paintings of Arcimboldo.

"You've never heard of Arcimboldo? Ignorant turds!

"He was the artist who did those pictures of men and women with faces made up of cleverly arranged flora and fauna.

"That's right, the fruit and veg guy . . . But don't forget the fish!

"Peter the Tenant read his invitation. It ran as follows: *You are cordially urged to come to Arcimboldo Hall tomorrow night to socialise among convivial coke heads with clothes based on one of his artworks.*

"There were no commas in this text. Poor Peter had to insert his own. He searched the sentence for a suitable place, finally choosing to plonk one between the word 'night' and the word 'to'. Then he prepared his costume, pinning bananas to his dressing gown, sewing plums and pomegranates onto a nightcap, utilising many kinds of fruit, but not kiwis, because he liked to shave those in private, and he felt he had none to spare: he needed at least a dozen for an explosively good wank. Similar to Mr Gum, your tutor, in many ways, was Peter the Tenant.

"Along to Arcimboldo Hall went he, and mighty weary when he arriveth, for 'twas a longish way forsooth, but entering into the spirit of things he opened a door and saw a table around which sat many figures composed of fruits, vegetables, fish, saucepans and other Arcimboldoesque elements.

"So he took his place and listened to the conversation, which mostly was about stalks and pips and bones, and he did his best to contribute wise and witty observations, and nobody resented his presence, and all in all he had a jolly good time, though deprived of the expected cocaine and oral sex.

"As he left the room he stripped off his costume, which was rapidly rotting away in stinky gloops of pap, but halfway across the lobby of the building he encountered a man in normal clothes who stopped him.

"Quothed this man, 'Hey, it's Peter the Tenant! Why are you so late?'

"Peter replied, 'I ain't late, I been at the party all night, dig? Whaddya mean with dat question, buster? Who the divil are you?'

"Came the retort, 'I'm the host of the party and rightful owner of this Hall and my name is not necessary to the anecdote. The coke-fuelled orgy took place in *this* room, not the one you came out of, but it's over now, I'm afraid. Actually I'm not afraid, I'm so full of coke I could bitchslap God."

"Peter sneered. 'You pulling my plonker, dude?

"The host shook his head. 'You came out of the room where we put the puppets, the costumes we made earlier, those inanimate works of art based on the models of the great Arcimboldo. Show me your invitation. I see, you put the comma in the wrong place. Let me correct it for you, like this:

" '*You are cordially urged to come to Arcimboldo Hall tomorrow night to socialise among convivial coke heads, with clothes based on one of his artworks.*

" 'That's right, amigo, you were supposed to come WITH clothes, not IN them, and because of one misplaced comma something supernatural happened! Now you are tainted with hellish essences and the aroma of vile evil!'

34

"He forbade Peter the Tenant from ever attending a cocaine night ever again! Never since has that sap sniffed snow.

"So let that be a warning to you, dear students, of how critical the precise placing of punctuation marks is. But I have a confession to make. Peter the Tenant in my tale was an impostor. He wasn't the man he claimed to be, but a dwarf in disguise! And when I say 'dwarf' I really mean *animated twat flap*. Its name is Hymen Simon, but that's not its real name, just what I call it.

"It was animated by a magical whistle after a young innocent girl had her virginity porked out of her. And here's another confession — that young girl was me! Yes, I often use a pseudonym when I travel, calling myself 'Primula'. This probably ties up some loose ends, and I like them tied up, especially when the knots dig hard into my flesh in sado-masochistic classroom games.

"Hey, what are you doing? Ripping open my blouse!

"Get your hands out of my panties, you goddam molesters! If you don't stop this at once I'll have to employ my teleportation device.

"That's right. An inventor by the name of Frabjal Troose gave it to me, enabling me to switch bodies with someone else.

"If you keep rustling inside my scrotum, searching for a quim that doesn't exist, I'll have no hesitation in employing the contraption.

"Right, you asked for it! Here goes! See the invisible flash?

"Bet your sodden cocks that made you blink!

"Hey . . . What's going on? Why am I tied up on the floor? Why are you abusing me with rough fingers in such a puerile fashion — aren't you aware that when so-called *satire* becomes too ambivalent, it supports the thing it's supposed to be attacking? Why haven't you chosen and utilised your favourite punctuation marks, as I requested? I'm Mr Gum, the Creative Writing tutor! Let me go at once! I'm not Mr Gmu pretending to be Lynne Truss anymore, I'm the real me! If you look closely you'll see that my cock resembles a big useful comma."

Canon Alberic's Photo-Album

"**I**F THERE'S ONE rule so important it's not really a rule but something as far beyond rules as amontillado is beyond sherry," said the Creative Writing tutor, "then that rule, even though it's not a rule, is *correct spelling*.

"Yes, my little chickadees, that's the money shot!

"Spell words wrong and you'll be marked for life as a fuckwit, make no mistake. But if you do make a mistake, don't spell it 'miztayk'.

"The chasm betwixt those two spellings is so enormous only a magical eye can peer across it. Not a magickal eye, take note!

"Once upon a time — as no story should ever begin in this day and age — there was a mad inventor by the name of Frabjal Troose. He ruled a city called Moonville, but that's not important right now, not as important as the fact that Frabjal's hobby was imparting conscious thought to inanimate objects.

"He achieved this with the aid of clockwork and electronics!

"He was so smart he could even impart conscious thought to abstract concepts. For instance he once grafted a mechanical brain onto the condition of 'disbelief' and set it free to roam his metropolis. His subjects began to doubt their own minds and probably would have gone crazy had it not been for the timely arrival of Lynne Truss, who was visiting the city in disguise. To express respect for Ms Truss I'll hereafter refer to her by her chosen pseudonym, Primula.

"Primula was walking down by the sea, a dry sea, very moony, when into sight came 'disbelief', running up the side of a crater. Like a pan in the flash — 'pan' is the Spanish word for 'bread' and to whip an exhibitionist's exposed meat with a baguette, whether seed sprinkled or not, requires speed — she reached into her panties and withdrew one of the correct punctuation marks she's always been in the habit of keeping down there and coshed 'disbelief' as it shot past her.

"Then she suspended 'disbelief' from her bracket . . .

"It's no less important for your readers to suspend disbelief — bear this in mind, you useless shits, if you want to be successful!

"Not that you ever *will* be successful. Cause you ain't as good as me, and I ain't been published, so how can you hope to be?

"Spell right, baby, you spell right . . . Once I was blind but now I see, now that you're in league with me, you made a believer out of me.

"Spell right, baby, you spell right . . .

"I think I've pressed the point firmly enough now.

"But just in case I haven't, let me tell you about Canon Alberic. Maybe some of you have heard of his scrapbook? It was famous for a time, among gay schoolboys and other incarcerated lackeys, but that was in the past and the past's another country. Having said that, other countries are getting more closely tied to our own, in economic and legal and political terms, at least in Europe, so that metaphor's a bit crap, but it wasn't originally mine, so I don't care overmuch.

"Where was I? Ah yes, the scrapbook of Canon Alberic. Well, even anachronisms move with the times, paradoxical as that might sound, and now there's a photo-album instead. I'll state the facts simply without blemish. Canon Alberic had an odd but very treasured hobby. He liked to take photographs of the most sentimental moments of the lives of every human being alive.

"Big job that, don't you agree? One wonders how the goddam hell he ever managed it, then one remembers this is a fictional story — a fictional tale within another fictional tale — and one grows mighty ashamed of wondering in the first place. If one is wise, one buttons one's lip after that, and I can't help noticing that several of the ladies present in my class tonight have buttoned lips, not to mention pierced noses and spinal tattoos. It's the modern way, is it? How bizarre. The present is another country, if you ask me. And if you're curious as to how I can see your noses *and* spines simultaneously, I'll respond with a single word: implausibility.

"In all my life I met only one man who ever met this Canon Alberic. His name is Mr Ugm and his story is a yarn of woe!

"Aye, that it is, me hearties, and for what it's worth here it is:

"Mr Ugm — no connection to me, of course — apart from the fact he *is* me — a minor detail — had an unusual childhood. Let's just say that his aunt liked to wear a strap-on and give him a good servicing from a young age. Maybe you believe he was a victim of perversion. But he never suffered from constipation in adulthood. Quite the opposite. Swings and roundabouts, with emphasis on the swings . . .

"Once in the garden when his parents were out shopping, his aunt came to Mr Ugm and what she did in the shade of a tree was remarkable. Mr Ugm never forgot it, even after he stopped limping. He considered it the defining moment of his existence, still does in some ways, even after being raped by a donkey on his eighteenth birthday, but that's another story and not for me to tell.

"Later, when he learned of the existence of Canon Alberic and his hobby, it occurred to him that a photo of *that* incident — the aunt, not the donkey: he had his own photos of the donkey — was in the photo-album!

"He yearned to get hold of that photo for three main reasons: firstly because it was a fixed image of a transient but very important sentimental moment, secondly because the photo might be used to blackmail him in the future and he wanted to prevent this from happening, thirdly because he needed fresh powerful wank material. He'd just bought a basket of kiwis and a packet of razors, as a matter of fact. So he decided to go in search of Canon Alberic and claim the photo!

"He made enquiries and learned that Canon Alberic presently resided in the south of France, oiling himself with truffle juice.

"Mr Ugm caught a passenger vessel to Biarritz — in fact he travelled on the back of Bryan the Ferry — and then set off inland to the

38

cathedral town where Canon Alberic's house shrugged its Gallic eaves nonchalantly.

"Mr Ugm's careful researches had revealed to him that Canon Alberic was prepared to hand over any photo from his album, but on one condition. The person who asked for a photo had to be prepared to kneel down and allow Alberic to shoot in their face. Those were the terms of the agreement.

"In some ways it would have been better for Mr Ugm if Bryan the Ferry had sunk in the middle of the Bay of Biscay and he'd drowned. But there had been nothing to indicate the voyage was doomed. No flaking paint on the hull, no rolling yellow fogs, no odd habits of the captain. Pity. But to return to my tale, my cautionary fable about the perils of spelling words incorrectly, I'll just state that Mr Ugm was more than happy for Canon Alberic to shoot in his face.

"After all, it wasn't the first time a holy man had come in his visage!

"No siree! Plenty of deacons, bishops, cardinals, had urged their thick cocks to spit over his eyes, nose, cheeks, lips, and they had accomplished this astonishing feat with odd hand manipulations, the like of which have rarely been seen. On one occasion an entire choir played bukkake with him in the nave of St Dangly's and he'd come away with increased cholesterol from the amount of boy yoghurt he'd unavoidably ingested during the process. As for lay brothers, I don't think there was one left he hadn't sucked off. So he wasn't worried in the slightest.

"He finally reached the town in question — St Bertrand de Comminges — and knocked with a ginger hand on the nutty wooden door. It swung open. There stood Canon Alberic. But there was a problem — he wasn't a man!

"No, he was a cannon, one of those big old guns that fire balls of iron.

"How can a cannon move of its own free will?

"He was one of Frabjal Troose's earlier experiments, of course!

"And the result of a terrible spelling mistake!

39

"Mr Ugm felt horribly depressed as he realised what was going to happen. First Canon Alberic would give him the photo in question, then he would light his fuse and blow Mr Ugm's head off his shoulders.

"There was time for a final request. 'Will you let me wank first?' Mr Ugm pleaded. 'The image of my aunt testing my sphincter to destruction will help me to explode my balls in a veritable Krakatoa of spunk!'

"Canon Alberic was a bit hard of hearing, because he was a cannon, not a man, and he only caught the first part of Mr Ugm's request. 'Sure I'll let you wank first. I'll call *first* right now, in fact. Hey first!'

"And into the room quickly bounded the abstract concept 'First' — also one of Frabjal Troose's creations. It was highly excited.

"It squeaked, 'Ain't never been wanked off before!'

"Mr Ugm sighed. He was suddenly too weary to argue with impossibilities. He did the deed that had to be done, earning first's eternal gratitude, and then he accepted the gift of the photo from Canon Alberic, but he had less than one second to enjoy it before Canon Alberic brutally shot in his face.

"Fortunately, or unfortunately, depending on how you look at it, Mr Ugm turned his head slightly at the same instant. He was trying to angle the photo in the light streaming through the window, to get a clearer image of the garden ravishment, and the cannonball passed through his right ear and came out of his left. And that's why he has the ears of a duchess's cunt. In case you were wondering.

"Did I forget to tell you that Mr Ugm became a Creative Writing tutor, just like me, and began living in my house and eating my food and being me in every way? I didn't tell you that? Then my secret's still safe!

"So remember: spelling words correctly is a matter of strange ears!

"This is the end of the lesson, chums, and the end of the class forever. I'm going to retire from teaching and start up a business with Fellatio Nelson. Not sure what we'll do yet, but I guess I'll find out to-

40

night, as I'm meeting him for a drink and a shanty, and maybe he'll extract his cock from my gut.

"Goodbye and take care, you dirty slimy fuckers!

"What, you want another story?

"I can't tell you new tales, I'm afraid, because I've run out of pseudonyms. My false names are made from shuffling the letters in my real name — Mr Gum — and this renders just five variations, because the word 'gum' only contains three letters, and I know this even though I don't teach maths! I have already pretended to be Mr Mug, Mr Mgu, Mr Umg, Mr Gmu and Mr Ugm.

"So sod off, and while you're at it, *dos* off, *dso* off, *ods* off, *sdo* off and *osd* off, into the bargain! I'd tell you to fuck off too, but there are too many variants and I'm tired. Just hop it, will ya? And provided you all come to bad ends and don't get published before me, good luck with your writing — and the same applies to you budding writers out there, reading this right now."

Up a Gumtree

The Groin Scratcher

H E WAS ENGLISH and he lived in a quaint old village and his name was Peter the Tenant and nobody ever suggested he was a sexual pervert. His erotic tastes were fairly normal: he was faithful to his girlfriend and fucked her twice a day and spurted his cream in her quim almost exclusively. On special occasions, such as his cock's birthday, he used her mouth and sprayed the back of her throat. Very rarely he wanked himself off between her tits but never did he penetrate her bumhole. In other words he was an unremarkable example of mister average and only the fact his cock was a different age to the rest of him betrayed his unique status among his fellow men.

He attended some of my creative writing classes and produced a few mediocre texts and that's high praise indeed coming from me, Mr Gum, the most vindictive and resentful tutor on the nightschool run, not that I play that game these days. No, I retired from teaching and went into business with Fellatio Nelson, a much more profitable affair, and I've never looked back, apart from those few occasions when implausible necessity compelled me to bend over without trousers. Yes I like to see what's coming in such situations. My business partner's style is quite different: he just likes to get his head down and not make eye contact with any mode of expression.

Did you appreciate that seemingly clever sentence? It's an example of my virtuosity in the art of arranging words in a straight line, a particular talent of mine, one you probably don't possess, and if you care to argue with that I'll set Fellatio Nelson on you. Then you'll be sorry and very sore. But there's no need for all this resentment and hostility, dear reader, so let's return to the issue of Peter the Tenant. He was born with a cock like any other man but dated its birth from his first erection, acquired while sliding down a banister at increasing velocity towards an ornamental knob at the terminus of the stairway. That's why man and dangly were different ages. The knob snapped off.

My own views on ornamental knobs are not widely known but I plan to write a short treatise on the subject in due course. One day the works of Mr Gum will dominate all other kinds of literature: just you wait! Anyway the penile dating system of Peter the Tenant had its own peculiar advantages and disadvantages, the listing of which might prove profitable but probably won't. His first erection occurred during his tenth summer. By the time Peter was twenty-five years old his cock was still underage for legal intercourse and any girl who introduced it into her quim was risking arrest. Having said that, how does one put handcuffs on a pussy? There must be a knack to it.

Luckily for all concerned, our unsynchronised hero has now passed his fortieth birthday and his girlfriend is only thirty, so cock and cunt are peers. Notice the subtle shift from past to present tense? You're such a genius, Mr Gum, yes I am. I might even shift the text into the future tense. Don't believe me? *You will* . . . Anyway, the girlfriend of our Peter was a sweet and willing conjuror's assistant by the name of Claribell Teddyface. We are all conjurors' assistants in this great illusion called life, but that's just metaphysical claptrap. Claribell was the real thing. She had assisted the Fructuous Grapevine on the cabaret circuit and picked up a few tricks from her master in the process.

If you've never heard of the Fructuous Grapevine, which is highly likely since I just invented him, don't bother seeking him out. His act wasn't worth the admission price, to say nothing of the fact that he died recently. Cows crushed him while he was walking between rural outposts of the aforementioned cabaret circuit. A cretinous farmer was listening to the radio and mistook the words of a Marvin Gaye song for a divine command. Without pausing to consider the awfulness of the pun and the damage it might do to *my* reputation when I related it, he calmly proceeded to 'herd it on the grapevine'. Bones splintered, blood

44

spurted, organs were squashed as flat as solid puddles of leaked tractor oil.

Without her master to pay her, and occasionally use her as a vessel for his seed, Claribell wandered in search of fresh opportunities. Somehow she met Peter the Tenant: I can't be bothered to invent the details of that encounter, so do it yourself if you think it necessary. Every morning and evening he came in her quim. I've already mentioned that, but I like the word 'quim' and have no scruples about repeating myself in order to write it again. If my name wasn't Mr Gum I would like to be called Sir Quim or something along those juicy lines. But let's not get deliciously distracted. Peter the Tenant was also a conjuror, an amateur but quite skilled, and so they were well matched in bed and elsewhere.

The first time they slept together turned out to be a magical occasion. He peeled off her clothes until she was left only in her panties but she restrained him from going further with the words "It's my time of the month" to which Peter responded "I don't really care". So the final item of clothing was removed, Claribell lay back with spread legs and reached down to pull the string that would remove her tampon. Out it came with a crimson slurp. Peter was about to plunge into the recently vacated space but Claribell rummaged inside and produced a second tampon, then a third and fourth. "Presto!" she cried each time. The tampons kept coming, like butchered bunnies out of a rubbery top hat. Soon there were a hundred of them.

Peter the Tenant waited impatiently for the trick to finish. When the last tampon was removed he clapped politely and threw himself on top of her. Cock slid into pussy like a mutilated hand into a deformed glove. Have you ever done that, dear reader? Mr Gum has: he's not a stinking virgin! That's me, by the way. Anyway, Peter panted these words into Claribell's ear: "Now I'm going to show you a trick of my own." And so he did. He began thrusting back and forth in the standard human manner, but on each thrust he slid his body up along hers. He was clearly using his cock to saw her in half along her longitudinal axis. What a sore puss saw pussy! She gasped while he rasped. Imperfect symmetry.

Eventually he reached the top of her head and the bisection was completed. He stood up, bone dust making him sneeze, and eased the two halves of her body apart. Then he walked around the bed, bowing to an invisible audience, before replacing the left and right sides. A few shakes of a bedsheet and some mumbled magic words and Claribell Teddyface was a whole woman again, though the incision never healed completely and still leaked pus whenever he brought her to orgasm. That was their inaugural fuck. And if you believe that, you really are a gullible gimp. No, of course it didn't happen that way. How could it? No man's cock is serrated, not even Marvin Gaye's, to say nothing of the fact that Claribell's pussy never opened without the correct security code.

That's right. Plunging straight into *her* quim is out of the question. A four-digit personal identification number has to be inputted before her labial lips juice up and part. Otherwise she remains clammed up tighter than a rusty singularity at the centre of an iron black hole. I can throw in some physics if I please: I'm Mr Gum! Now then. Claribell whispered the relevant code to Peter the Tenant and he told it to me and I don't mind passing it to you right now. It went like this: clockwise tongue lick on the left nipple, ditto on the right, middle finger in the belly button, knuckle rap on the pubic bone. Do that and you're in. Peter did it often, always with a backward glance to make sure nobody was spying on the sequence.

One evening the procedure felt different from normal, slightly strange, the nipples a little rougher, the belly button less deep, the pubic bone more metallic. But he didn't take much notice because her quim opened for him without fuss. In he went, humped the required number of times, ejaculated. Then he rolled over and fell asleep. All night he was plagued by involuntary orgasms of horrendous intensity and duration. He woke in a sweat, inputted the security code, fucked Claribell again, but this morning his sperm was less creamy and deployed into her pussy with less power. The day began properly. The involuntary orgasms continued, dwindling in force, disappearing for good in the late afternoon. Peter the Tenant limped back home. A curious emptiness clanged wetly inside his soul like a bell with a tampon clapper.

The evening passed unremarkably with his girlfriend. Then it was bedtime. He threw her down on the sheets, applied the security code, slid in and pumped. But nothing came. Try as he might, no sperm emerged. Finally he had to pull out and make his apologies. Claribell was tolerant but when the same thing happened in the morning she couldn't hide her annoyance. "I'm going through a dry patch," Peter gasped, "so give me some time to get over it." Yes, Claribell was happy to do that. But the sperm never returned. Peter modified his diet to increase his potency: he ate ginseng salads with horny goat weed garnish and Spanish Fly dressing. But his tanks never refilled. Finally he rang the local branch of his sperm bank to check his account.

"You are clean out of come," came the reply.

"But I had enough spunk in there to last a lifetime! How has my account been drained? I limit myself to two fucks a day," protested Peter.

"Not according to the data on the screen in front of me," the anonymous voice insisted. "It seems you spent all your savings in just twelve hours. Fifty gallons went on a bukkake competition, another twenty on spit-roasting, ten on glory holes, another ten on prostrate milking and the final ten on erotic asphyxiation. That makes one hundred gallons in total, the upper limit of your lifetime allowance. Sir, you have been fucked."

"But how could this happen? None of those orgasms were mine!"

"Clearly you are the victim of fraudsters. Sometimes they fit false erogenous zones over a man's girlfriend that look just like the real thing. That's how they get access to personal identification codes. You need to be alert for anything unusual when operating a lady's nipples and clitoris. This is a common problem for sperm banks. Don't panic.

47

You might not have lost all your spunk forever. Maybe we can reimburse you."

Hope glittered in Peter's eyes. "Really? How?"

"We need to take some personal details, sir. Firstly, may I have your date of birth?"

"Certainly. 24ᵗʰ November 1954."

"Hmm . . . ah! Well yes . . . but . . . I'm sorry, that's not the date I have listed under your cock's signature. There's quite a discrepancy . . . "

"Wait! It's easily explained. My cock's birthday is different from my own. Let's see. 2ⁿᵈ July 1964. Just before teatime. On the banister. Is that right? Please don't hang up!"

A flicker of movement violated the edges of Peter's vision. He turned to confront Claribell who had packed a suitcase and was preparing to leave. "This pussy needs milk!" she sneered before storming out the door. All was lost. Peter hesitated between girlfriend and telephone. Then he raised the mouthpiece and said, "I want to close my account. I don't need it anymore." But the tone was already dead.

To prove I'm a man of integrity and courage as well as enormous talent, I ought to confess that Peter the Tenant doesn't really exist, or rather he *does* exist but isn't who he claims to be. His real name is Hymen Simon and he's a dwarf or animated puppet made from a burst maidenhead. He played a vile trick on me once and this is my revenge: telling the world about the time his balls went dry forever.

In fact I was the one responsible for draining them. With plenty of help from Fellatio Nelson, of course. I told you we went into business together but I never specified our work was *legal*, did I? Not at all! In fact we are fraudsters, the pair of us, and we specialise in fitting false erogenous zones on female bodies. Getting access to those bodies is the difficult part. I knock on doors like a regular salesman and offer the services of the finest Creative Writing tutor in history. While the housewives are distracted by my banter, Fellatio Nelson skilfully attaches the fake zones. He's good at that, stealthy as a snake: probably because he once had a serpentine cock. I broke that in another story. Things other than banister knobs do snap off, you know.

I've lost count of the number of personal security codes we've managed to obtain in this devious manner, spending the seed of other men on our own sexual experiences. An endless supply of sperm is ours for the spurting. But I regard the theft of Peter the Tenant's entire stock of jism as my most malicious, and therefore greatest triumph. Left without a girlfriend he would have turned to masturbation for solace. But without cream to spill, what is the point of wanking? His solitary erotic pleasure now consists of obsessively scratching his groin with un-cut fingernails.

This possibly puerile incident happened in the charmingly sordid village of Precome-on-Bum.

Plop Fiction

ESPERADOES LIVE IN desperate times. Just as Victorians lived in the Victorian Age. That's common sense. And desperate times require desperate measures. Everyone is familiar with that saying.

Both my business partner and myself are desperadoes, so I summoned him to my office to discuss the ramifications. Fortunately I work from home and my office is the lounge of the house I share with him, and he was sitting on the sofa at the time, right next to me in fact, thus it didn't take him long to respond to my urgent call.

"What's up?" he asked from the corner of his mouth.

"Dear Fellatio," I began, "please don't be so blasé. We are possibly on the verge of a crisis. Until a moment ago I knew all our basic needs: power, wealth, physical immortality, universal acknowledgement of our true worth, an ability to mimic great apes. But now it's clear we must add 'desperate measures' to the list. Yet I can't even guess what those are."

"Have no fear, my gummy chum, for I'll do the guessing for you," he replied.

"I wish you wouldn't refer to me like that," I sighed.

"I don't grant wishes, but I'll endeavour to be more thoughtful in future. You are none other than Mr Gum, once the finest Creative Writing tutor in the cosmos, a man whose warnings against plot spoilers should be printed on every bag that hasn't had the cat let out of it. I am Fellatio Nelson, your friend and erstwhile sodomiser, and together we are a pair of fraudsters who specialise in identity theft for the purpose of making unauthorised withdrawals from sperm banks."

"Thanks for that unnecessary resumé," I said, "but let's return to the original point. Desperadoes live in desperate times. We are desperadoes. Desperate times require desperate measures. Therefore *we* require desperate measures. But what in the name of cocksucking are they?"

Fellatio frowned, shifted his eyepatch from left to right peeper, switched amputations from dexter to sinister hand, rotated the bicorn hat atop his head by sixty-nine degrees. He always does that when preparing for a confrontation of some sort. Needless to say I was a little worried. Having said that, if it's needless to say then I don't have to say it, and if I don't say it, how can it exist? This is fiction, not real life, and anything unsaid here doesn't have any real substance or significance.

So I wasn't worried in the slightest.

But Fellatio doesn't give a damn about logic. He once captained a ship whose seamen were entirely composed of discharged semen, congealed. There was a lot of gloopy furling and unfurling on *that* voyage but nothing remotely logical. And so the seeds of our very worst argument were sprayed onto the tissue of lies that fills the pocket of our lives.

"Whatever desperate measures are," intoned Fellatio, "they obviously come in pints."

"You archaic blubbering buffoon!" I wailed. "How can you remain unaware of modern units of liquid capacity? I'll wager the root of my cock that desperate measures are issued in litres."

"You gibbering man-whore! You gingivitis of the personality! You are so boring that when you enter a cabin it feels as if an interesting person has just left. You are so ugly that when a windmill . . . "

"Litres!" I barked.

"Pints!" he shrieked.

There was only one acceptable way of settling the matter: compromise. I bet you thought we were going to fight a duel? Sure you did. Assume that Fellatio and I are a rather immature pair, don't you? Just because we like juvenile humour and indulge in infantile behaviour doesn't mean we aren't normal grown ups. Does an orchard deny its own pips? Don't poop your pants while you work that one out.

"How exactly shall we compromise?" asked Fellatio.

I pondered the issue. "How about if we jointly agree to choose a unit of measurement that is neither metric nor imperial?"

"Bravo, Mr Gum! What a capital idea. Not a day passes when I don't thank my lucky quasars I'm a character in the same story as you, written by you, with all my dialogue scripted beforehand for maximum efficiency. How I would like to wank you off to express my gratitude!"

I smirked to myself. I wrote the original draft of this story in pencil, so I'm able to rub out anything I don't like and replace it with something more to my taste. The speech you've just read wasn't Fellatio's real reply. That may sound dishonest, but so what? I'm Mr Gum, a master of the stealthy but thorough revision, so organised about my re-writes that even the cardinal points on the weather vane on my roof have been edited.

Which reminds me: I tried to push the manuscript of my first completed novel under the front door of a famous London publisher, but it wouldn't fit. I revised the entire book, cutting material, but it was still too thick. A third rewrite didn't help matters, nor a fourth. The fifth and sixth fared no better. I finally realised the book would never slide under, no matter how many pages I deleted, because the door was fitted with draft excluders.

Wind. That's the connection between vanes and novels, in case you're still wondering. But I merely turned to Fellatio with the words:

"Go on then, but make it quick."

Almost a minute later, I buttoned my trousers and continued our earlier conversation while he wiped his fingers on one of the cushions. "How about tubs or barrels as a measurement unit?"

He soothed his aching wrist by rubbing it with juice from his amputation. "Not bad. But we're grandiose fellows, especially you, and I can't help feeling that if we're lacking a fundamental, it ought to be a big one."

52

"I agree. Maybe our desperate measures are equivalent to reservoirs?"

"That's more like it, laddie! So let's go out and get some! Why are we waiting? I say we do a good old-fashioned hold-up on a sperm bank today."

"To be honest, dear Fellatio, I'm disinclined to take such risks. We're doing well with our scam of fitting false erogenous zones over ladies and draining the sperm bank accounts of their boyfriends and casual lovers. In the past six months we've stolen an average of 500 gallons of spunk every week to spend on our own sexual experiences. Do we really need more than that?"

"Gallons! That's an imperial unit! I win the root of your cock! Hand it over at once."

"I refuse!" I spat through clenched teeth.

A strange light came into his eyes and he shook his head slowly, his bicorn hat not moving thanks to its gyroscopic styling. "I already took it as advance payment when I wanked you off."

I didn't need to lower my trousers again to confirm the truth of his awful assertion. "Bah!"

"I'll transplant it to my own groin. Then I'll have a replacement for the one you snapped off."

I pretended not to care. "Dear Fellatio, I haven't spurted my own cream for months, not since we went into business together as fraudsters. It's all the same to me. Besides, my ears are shaped like a Duchess's cunt and your mocking aristocratic laughter just gives me aural orgasms, so who's the real winner, buster?"

He had inserted one arm down the side of the sofa, rummaging around like a cow with its hoof up a vet's arse, grimacing as he did so, until he finally found what he was looking for.

"I had an idea they fell down here," he said.

"My ears?" I gasped.

"No, *these*, silly," he answered.

Two flintlock pistols. Studded with melted toffees and quasi-fungal with fluff, they reclined in Fellatio's lap like a pair of half-cocked mutant clitorises. I suddenly realised that nothing could now deter my friend from robbing a sperm bank the direct way. True, the potential profits were massive, putting the gains of our present operation in a rancid-milky sort of shade, but there was also a vastly inflated chance of apprehension and punitive confinement.

"Are you with me?" he abruptly demanded.

If I declined, the root of my cock would be lost forever, so my options were severely limited. "All for Gum and Gum for all!" I cried.

"I'll take that for a yes," he grinned.

For reasons he never made clear, there was no time to be lost. We couldn't find a pair of stockings to pull over our heads, so we borrowed a method used by ladies during wartime shortages, drawing the webs of the tarty leggings on our faces with a pencil and using each other's expressions as mirrors. When we had finished we were unrecognisable as ourselves for it appeared we had swapped identities.

"By all the merry tritons of the deep," cursed Fellatio softly, "you look like a rapist of paedophiles."

"And you like a genius!" I retorted.

"No more perfect disguise for a duo exists! Take up your pistol, Mr Gum. Our Bentley car waits in the garage to convey us. I say we should rob the largest available branch of the most successful sperm bank in existence."

"You mean Wank Mutual in Debauchester?"

"At the risk of being criticised for massive puerility, yes. Get your sneakers on, Mr Gum, we're a different kind of criminal now. Thugs. That's what we are. Tie up your laces, laddie me boy. Double bows. Now get this into your academic head: no referring to me by my real name. And vice versa. We'll use code names based on, say, colours. I'll be Mr Mauve and you can be Mr Puce. Then when we . . . "

"Why am I Mr Puce? Why can't we pick our own colours?"

"No way. It doesn't work. You'll get both of us fighting over who gets to be Mr Vermilion with Indigo Stripes. So you're Mr Puce. Be thankful you're not Mr Spaut, Mr Onk or Mr Cheen — those are colours that no longer exist in the visible spectrum. They fell out."

"But Mr Puce is a little too close to Mr Vomit."

"Then move away from him! What's *he* doing here anyway? This is a private residence. He'd better have a damn good reason . . . "

"How about Mr Lavender? That sounds good, I'll be Mr Lavender."

"You're not Mr Lavender. Some ladyboy who sings at Club Cockring in Stiffy-on-Tickle is Mr Lavender. You're Mr Puce!"

"With respect," I interrupted with one of my smuggest smiles. "I think that colours have been overused in the operation you are plotting. I recommend code names based on other systematic categories."

"Like smells, you mean? Or sounds? Or tastes?"

I shrugged. "How about oral reactions to ejaculation? I can be Mr Spit, you can be Mr Swallow . . . "

"Very well. The other thing to remember is not to drop Creative Writing tips while we're on the job. I love your lectures as much as the next man, whoever the hell he is, hopefully he's not Mr Vomit, but your distinctive teaching methods will betray your identity. We go in hard, snatch the come and get out fast. Wham, bam, thank you ma'am!"

"My favourite kind of plan," I conceded.

"A man, a plan, a sperm bank — wanker!" cried Fellatio in joy, misquoting a palindrome that was also inappropriate. But his glee was infectious and I found myself chuckling along. His gun was in my hand and I aimed it at the ceiling to fire a celebratory shot but my companion shook a finger.

"They have to be reloaded after every shot and we're running low on gunpowder. Save it."

I therefore unbuttoned his trousers and fired a different kind of celebratory shot. It took a long time to effect the discharge and the force wasn't quite great enough. The pearly dum-dum didn't splatter the plaster above our heads but arced across the room, landing on the television. The reason we were sitting side by side on the sofa was because we were watching the news but suddenly there was a shower of sparks and a loud pop and the screen went dead.

"Your spunk has fused the set!" I roared.

"*My* spunk?" he grimaced. "This is your cock, not mine. At least the root is yours. My own broke off, as well you know, many colons ago. Clearly you're some kind of monstrous dullard, for you subjected your tool to a second wank before it was ready. That's why you couldn't hit the ceiling. You'll have to get it fixed tomorrow . . . "

I was genuinely confused. "The cock or the ceiling?"

"The television!" he roared, rolling his eyes in vicious exasperation. "Let's waste no more time on banter, my lad, but put our little scheme into effect immediately. Before the day is over we'll be swimming in man mayonnaise, make no mistake! Go and fetch the hose from the shed while I load the electric pump into the Bentley. Any final questions?"

"Just one. What do windmills do because I'm so ugly?"

"Reverse the direction of their spin, turning flour back to grain, deluging marshes that have already been drained, returning the wind to the place it came from. And all because you're a grotesque lubber!"

"Glad we got that cleared up . . . "

"No problem. Now then: ¡Vamos! I say it in Spanish because I know you once lived in Madrid. It means *let's go* in case you lied about learning some of the lingo, which wouldn't be untypical behaviour of you. Look out the window and tell me what you see. An arid dusty crater bottom, eh? Well we're going to flood this geological depression to its lip with testicle milk. I guess we'll have to relocate to the top floor of the house but that's no hardship for desperadoes."

"I wonder if we might have missed the point about desperate measures?" I ventured uneasily.

Fellatio Nelson was in no mood for a rethink. "No, I don't believe so. Come on, we're still wasting time!"

While we made our final preparations for the heist and boarded the Bentley, me in the passenger seat, my friend behind the wheel, and growled off to our destination, with hastily falsified number plates, I might as well fill you in on some details about our place of residence. We occupied a deserted mansion that once belonged to Frabjal Troose. After he left Moonville on his first voluntary exile, he sought refuge on the shore of a large lake, had it drained to resemble a lunar sea and raised a huge house on the dried out bottom.

It has been rumoured by certain buffoons that his first exile was spent inside a volcano, within Mount St Dangly's to be precise, that legendary rock phallus I suspect to be no more than a geologist's erotic fantasy. Certainly there were no volcanoes anywhere in the region. I had climbed to the roof of the mansion to ascertain this, looking in all directions and perceiving no cones on any horizon, neither smoking nor dormant. But tall tales about Frabjal Troose multiply like rumouring buffoons, which is logical enough, and there's nothing I can do to stop them. Better not even to try.

Frabjal dwelled here for several years before an urge to travel seized hold of him. Off he went with a couple of bags on a journey that eventually took him back to Moonville, after he founded a dozen other cities dedicated to Earth's cheesy satellite on the way. But he never returned to his mansion and so we now regarded it as entirely our own property, which perhaps wasn't a wise thing to do with something connected to that tyrant. No matter. Life isn't worth living if you can't incur a wrath or two. Not even fictional life.

The mansion was too big for our needs and the idea of dwelling just at the top suited me fine. I used one room as storage space for my unpublished manuscripts and Fellatio claimed another as a shrine to the figureheads of his previous schooners. A third was a laboratory where we experimented with shibari and other forms of exotic bondage. We also had a guest room in permanent preparation for the spontaneous arrival (or generation) of Lynne Truss, but we never really expected her to

57

turn up. The fifth room we used was the lounge and the sixth was our bedroom.

The main reason we spent so much time watching the news was to catch the weather reports at the end. Rain is a more serious than average threat to people who live inside a waterproof crater . . .

Frabjal Troose, I hardly need remind you, is dedicated to the moon and he also happens to be a mad inventor of extraordinary skill. He once devised a kind of invisible ray that would pull the moon closer to the Earth because he wanted to marry the moon, but the device that projected the ray was knocked off its alignment and it ended up pointing at Saturn instead, which revolves on the same ecliptic as the moon, as do all the planets, and the rings of that world were dislodged and pulled through space towards us like an oncoming doughnut of subzero nebular material. Not tasty.

That was an aside. Do you like my asides? Come back for more when you're ready. Always upfront about them, me. See what I did then? Front, back, sides: three spatial dimensions for the price of one. I'm Mr Gum!

Now our Bentley is speeding across the parched floor of the dusty bowl towards the series of curves that will take us over the rim and towards Debauchester where the largest sperm bank in existence waits for us on Wet Patch Street. I look forward to skirting those quaint urban labyrinths known as Organ-in-Cider, Stiffy-on-Tickle and Precome-on-Bum. The indigenous inhabitants of the region hold strange festivals that involve excessive amounts of pickle. Not my problem. While Fellatio puts his foot down hard on the accelerator, I feed out hosepipe behind us. Soon we are climbing out of the cosmic punch mark, for that's how I regard all craters. The Earth frequently gets fisted from outer space, it's a fact.

"Dear Fellatio, I mean Mr Swallow," I call into his ear, "do you know the shortest route to our destination?"

"Why have you drifted into the present tense?" he answers.

58

I cringe before performing the necessary corrections. "Sorry. How's the tense now? Any better?"

"I believe so, Mr Gum, I mean Mr Spit," he said.

And so we were back on course again, hurtling up the rough track to the rim. On the other side was a steep long slope and the descent was scary but when we reached the bottom we began heading west across the flats towards civilisation, and gradually the twisted desert landscape turned into less arid scrubland and then lush meadows. We passed through the Forest of Humping and emerged into what was almost a pastoral paradise, where the bulk of the inbred population cooled big ears and soothed fingertips lacerated by too many banjo strings in a brace of ancient and molester-friendly villages.

We drove into one and parked near a row of shops. Fellatio urged me out of the car. "We don't have many bullets and it's surely a good idea to get some now. The bank staff might resist."

I adjusted the pencil stocking on my face — it was too tightly drawn — and eased myself out of the Bentley. Then I strolled casually along the street. Which shop should I enter to buy ammunition? The first in the row sold hunting gear, the second was a bakery, the third a milliner's. I made my choice, entered and emerged with a box tied up with a red ribbon. Fellatio released the handbrake and we continued on our way.

"The name of this village is What-a-Twat," I informed him. "That's what the shopkeeper said when he saw me."

"Don't engage with the locals if you can avoid it," snapped Fellatio. "The fewer witnesses, the better."

"Nonetheless the information is useful," I sniffed as I flappingly struggled with a large road map.

"Listen closely, Mr Gum, I mean Mr Spit, it's not in our interest to get there by the most direct route. Even with the electric pump running at full power it will take many hours to drain the vaults under the bank. A suspicious citizen in the vicinity might notice our hose and call the police: those official busybodies will then have no trouble following the

59

direction of the hosepipe until they chance on our house. Much better to weave randomly all over the place until we reach Debauchester by accident. That's one sure way of muddling the issue and throwing investigators off the scent!"

I accepted the logic of this and hurled the map out the window. "Quite right, dear Fellatio, I mean Mr Swallow . . . "

"Why did you do that?" he wailed.

"Because it's a hindrance, not a help," I responded.

"You moron! A discarded map lying in a roadside ditch is an obvious clue that criminals are planning to get lost on the way to a crime scene. I just hope the police don't find it there. We can't afford to make such mistakes!"

"That's the last one, I assure you. I'm Mr Spit, I mean Mr Gum, and I always get stuff right."

He narrowed his eyes. "Sure you do. Just make sure it's the best sort of right. Now then, keep reeling out that hose. There's probably a long way to go. Let's turn right at this junction, shall we? How about left after that? The stormclouds in these parts have rather an odd aspect, almost as if they have been turned upside-down before delivery into the sky."

I said nothing. We were already lost: fair enough. But I also knew that Fellatio's strategy could generate its own disadvantages. For instance we might break down and not know *which* nowhere's middle had claimed us, or we might wander completely off the edge of the map and end up in a foreign land where any spunk we robbed would have to be converted back into *pounds spermling* at a loss. Still, that wasn't my fault. Fellatio would have to shoulder, stomach and groin the responsibility.

The day dragged on. We spotted a sign for the hamlet of Grind-My-Bones but the mileage was missing. I wanted to discharge my pistol at it: I wanked Fellatio off instead. He almost skidded off the road at the crucial moment. Odd coincidence, because none of his spunk went under the tyres. It all remained inside the vehicle. Blobs of come

60

glistened on the knob of the gearstick and neither of us knew how they got there. Had the handle had its own orgasm?

Already the light was fading. Very little hosepipe remained on the reel. Our heist had already failed, or so it seemed. Then we turned a corner and rattled over a little stone bridge. Suddenly we were in Debauchester, its amber coloured buildings looming over us like rows of church musicians drunk on scrumpy. We passed the castle, bounced down a cobbled incline, jerked to a halt on the corner of Wet Patch and Whiplash Streets. We checked our weapons and nodded to each other.

"Come, let's go!" Fellatio hissed.

"Which one do you prefer?" I asked.

"What do you mean?"

"Shall we 'come' or shall we 'go'? We can't do both. They are opposite concepts," I explained.

"Bloody hell, Mr Gum, I mean Mr Spit, didn't you hear what I said about not dropping Creative Writing tips? You really are the limit."

I accepted the rebuke. "Yes, I'm the limit of excellence. But if you want my opinion, I suggest we go rather than come. After all, we've only just got here and the bank will be closing any moment now."

"Hurry up then, you fungoidal fuckwit!"

Fellatio is a clever fellow but not as intelligent or resourceful as me. I had already broken off the rear-view mirror and was holding it up to his face when he spoke the preceding words and so his insult was directed at himself. He may be the bee's knees but I'm the octopus's elbows — or is it the other way around? Anyway, the verbal rebound caught him full in the mush and I used his stunned reaction to reassert control over the group.

"Look lively, you shanty sucker, there's a sperm bank to rob! In my wake, daddy-o!"

And I was running towards the slowly closing door of Wank Mutual with Fellatio stamping along behind me. I held the end of the hose in one hand, the beribboned box in the other, my pistol tucked into my belt. Fellatio lumbered after with the electric pump. I reached the threshold before he did and inserted my foot into the gap, but the mechanism was automatic and continued to shut despite the relatively minor obstacle of my shoe-encased toes. I do believe those more southerly fingers of mine would have been crushed to a pinkish pulp, a substance from which a low grade paper might be manufactured, not suitable for the main body of a text but perfectly adequate for footnotes, had not Fellatio discharged his gun through the gap at a lever on the wall inside the bank. When the smoke cleared the door swung open by itself and we squeezed through.

There was no point bluffing our way to the counter where a single receptionist blinked at us in exasperation. I absorbed all details of the scene at once. Behind her stood two clerks and a sallow manager and none were terrified: a bad sign. We already had stockings on our faces and had forgotten to bring lifelike masks to wear over them, so it was essential to move fast. Fellatio and I hurtled to the counter and cried:

"Anybody move and we'll plug 'em!"

The manager managed to speak without moving his lips. "With respect, none of us are leaking."

"Wise guy, huh?" I snarled.

"Why yes," he replied, "which is why I was given this job. I always *manage* to do stuff, hence I am a *manager*. My salary reflects my competence in this regard. If I merely coped with situations I would be a coper: a man who makes barrels. I do no such thing!"

"That's a cooper, you dolt!" I screeched. "Get your spelling right or I'll mark you severely down."

He frowned and I heard Fellatio's sharp intake of breath. "For fuck's sake, Mr Gum, I mean Mr Spit, you're not a Creative Writing tutor: you're an armed rober, I mean robber. Don't you understand?"

I digested these words. "A mean robber. Not a nice one, not at all. So shut the fuck up, Mr Manager — I won't say anything about split infinitives at this point — and insert the end of this hose into your vaults."

"Be smart about it," added Fellatio.

"With respect to this gentleman's request," the manager answered, nodding at me, "I'm afraid I must decline because you ordered all of us not to move. Obeying you now will violate your previous command. As for being smart about it, haven't you noticed how carefully ironed my shirt is, how beautifully knotted my tie?"

Fellatio turned to me and licked his sweaty lips. "We won't get anywhere with this guy, it's clear as authentic female ejaculate he's going to stall us until the end of time. But the other members of staff will be more accommodating after this smartass gets a cap popped in it."

"I beg your pardon?" I whispered.

"Don't act dumb, Mr Gum, I mean Mr Spit. My pistol is empty, yours is loaded. Take this jerkoff and pop a cap in his ass. What's the matter? You don't speak movie? I thought you were a master of fictional dialects including Script."

"And so I am, dear Fellatio, I mean Mr Swallow, but I want to make it just as clear as you did I'm not a Creative Writing tutor. No, I'm a professional thug. So yes, I'll pop a cap in his ass, and in fact your request affords me some relief with respect to the choice of shop I made earlier, for I confess I was worried about that awhile back. But this receptionist is a girl and I don't want to expose her virginal eyes — maybe her cunt's been wedged open with cock meat but I'm sure her pupils haven't — to such a scatological scene."

"By all the dried plums of Shropshire, you're a prune, I mean prude, Mr Gum, I mean Mr Spit!" roared Fellatio, I mean Mr Swallow, as he lowered the electric pump to the floor and connected it to the hosepipe.

"Perhaps so," I conceded. "All the same there's probably a backroom I can use for the operation."

"I don't really care where you do it," grumbled Fellatio, his cheeks glowing like the buttocks of the sun. "Just pop a cap in this motherfucker's ass, will ya?"

"Aye aye, my cocksucking accomplice!" I cried, determined to restore jollity to the situation.

"Go on then!" he bellowed. "While you do the popping, I'll lower the hose into the vault."

I nodded and eased myself over the low counter, my trousers ripping as I performed the feat, then I beckoned at the manager with my pistol. "After you, chum."

He moved very reluctantly. "Where are you taking me? You won't get away with this. Wank Mutual has never been successfully robbed. We're the cream of the sperm banks and always protect our customers' deposits."

"Do him before he triggers any alarms," barked Fellatio. "This wiseguy is some kind of know-it-all."

"No fear of that. A popping of one cap in one ass is imminent," I reassured my companion.

Opening a nearby door, I pushed the manager inside. The room beyond was an unusual kind of broom cupboard, so large it was equipped with desk, chair, lamp, telephone, computer, filing cabinet, the lingering smell of a regularly fucked secretary, and even a sign that said: MANAGER'S OFFICE. People who work in banks are eccentric, no lie. I ordered the imbecile to remove his trousers and underpants and get down on all fours. Then I untied the ribbon on my box . . .

Because events took a dramatic turn for the worse from this point, I deem it more seemly to relate subsequent incidents, at least for a paragraph or two, from a more distant perspective. Indeed, I might even step outside that surreal broom cupboard for a moment and allow the prose of this tale to hang around with Fellatio Nelson while he attempted to force the lady receptionist and the two clerks to show him where to insert the end of the hose. Until it was safely in all the way, he couldn't begin pumping.

He trained his empty gun on those hapless lackeys of the multinational masturbation markets, trusting that folks who trade in spunk all day wouldn't know blanks from live rounds, and insisted on being shown the access hatch to the vaults. This confrontation was made less deadly than it ought to have been because of a peculiar distraction: a grunting and squeaking coming from behind the closed door of the room into which I had taken the manager.

These sound effects increased in volume and soon were accompanied by panting, gasping and a few moans of a pain that was also a forbidden pleasure. Fellatio later swore he heard me mutter 'That's right, all the way up, you man bitch' but I suspect he's exaggerating for effect, though precisely for *what* effect remains a mystery. He was forced to stop harassing his victims and wait for my return. But the expected detonation of my pistol never came. Instead the grunting merely turned into a thin scream with overtones of squelching. Finally he could bear it no longer and leaped over the counter, seizing the handle of the door and glaring back at his three captives with these words:

"Any of you goes for an alarm and I'll wash my armpits with your prostrate glands!"

They nodded meekly and Fellatio flung the door open. The sight that confronted him caused his bushy eyebrows to curl and his amputation to grow back. The manager was still on all fours. I had almost succeeded in getting all of it up him: only part of the brim still protruded. I worked with just the middle finger of my right hand, with short stabbing motions, easing the accessory into the tight hole with minimum but still considerable fuss.

"What the hell are you doing?" Fellatio roared.

"What I was told to do," I answered without looking up. "Popping a cap in this swine's ass."

"That's a Mexican hat," observed Fellatio.

"Well yes, they didn't have any caps, that milliner's shop, only sombreros. But I've nearly popped it up him good. The sun won't shine out of there again: even if it does, such an expansive example of functional headwear will ensure his rectum's forever in a sartorial shade."

"You fucking useless tosser," breathed Fellatio.

"No need for that!" I protested, rather hurt at his tone of voice. "The procedure I've just successfully carried out isn't an easy one. Look at the damage done to my finger! It's covered in brown smelly blood and even though there's no pain or other physical indication of a wound I can't deny the evidence of my own eyes and nose."

"Mr Gum, I mean Mr Swallow, no that's me, I mean Mr Spit," intoned Fellatio in his coldest voice, fury moving through his veins like icebergs flushed into a sewer system, "let me ask you an essential question: are you an American?"

"Why no, buddy," I responded truthfully.

"In that case there should have been no misunderstanding. I asked you to pop a cap in his ass, not his *arse*. What's an ass in our own non-Yankee culture? That's right, a donkey. I expected you to insert headwear into this wiseguy's beast of burden. All managers of sperm banks own one, it's a hallowed tradition from long ago. They aren't permitted to travel to work by any other method. Instead of doing that, you experimented with his anus, wasting valuable time."

I gazed around the room, scrutinizing every nook, cranny and niche. "There aren't any donkeys here, not a single one, so your criticism is a little unjust."

"It's in the car park," gasped the manager, drool pouring down his chin. "You don't think I'd keep a braying quadruped in my office, do you? I park it in a reserved space outside. A sperm bank isn't a stable!"

Fellatio frowned more closely at the manager, then he tapped me on the shoulder and pointed. But I was still trying to think of ways I might redeem myself. "Shall I extract the sombrero and transfer it to the interior of the donkey? Or I could leave this hat where it is and borrow a beret from a passing bohemian. I'll do anything to . . . "

Fellatio continued pointing with such rigidity and formal hatred that my voice dwindled away and I finally squinted at what he was trying to show me. One of the manager's arms was outstretched and his fully extended finger was pressing down hard on a silent buzzer fixed to the floor. I rolled my eyes and suddenly realised that the entire room was full of similar alarms, secretive little buttons positioned in unexpected places, designed to enable a captive to summon help no matter what bizarre contortions he was forced to perform.

"How long has he been doing that?" Fellatio demanded.

I gulped painfully. "His position hasn't altered since I started forcing the hat into him, maybe twenty minutes ago."

"Enough time for the police to get here and surround the place," sighed Fellatio.

"Robber scum like you deserve the harshest penalty," croaked the manager. He finally removed his digit from the buzzer and turned his head to grin sickly at me. "I'll never be able to sit down at normal dinner parties ever again — only at events where the wearing of headgear is encouraged, and I don't get invited to many of those. I hope they lock you up in a prison ship and throw away the quay!"

"Only if they take us alive . . . " sneered Fellatio.

"Let's get out of here. Forget the spunk and run!" I cried.

"Maybe it's too late for that," warned Fellatio. "Go to the window and tell me what you see. Maybe we can sneak out the back way but I'm not too hopeful about that."

I stepped quickly to the rear of the room and peeped through the glass pane. Behind the parked cars and the tethered donkey, among the thorn bushes, dark blue shapes flitted like solidified tears. I reported this spectacle to Fellatio. He cursed and chewed the fingernails of his real hand.

"Back out the way we came in?" I suggested.

Muffled shouts from the street and the wail of a badly maintained megaphone demonstrated that both escape routes were already cut off. "Dip into your mind for your siege mentality!" advised Fellatio.

"We can hold them off indefinitely here, this place is constructed like a fortress," I remarked.

67

The manager sniggered. He was still drooling but the glee in his voice was dry and brittle, not watery at all. He moved painfully, keeping to all fours, and clearly his mind was on the verge of snapping, for his eyes pointed in different directions and his two nostrils quivered at different speeds. "But you left my clerks and receptionist unattended in the lobby. They will have opened the front door. Your fortress is already broached and your testicles are as good as poached!"

Fellatio stepped forward and cuffed the moron with the back of his amputation. Then he cocked his head. Shouts and stamping boots outside the door confirmed the truth of the manager's vindictive words. We were both truly shafted. I was too scared to react in any way: I just stood there in a casual pose, my fake nonchalance spurring my companion to take desperate action. He seized me by the collar and dragged me across the room.

"Quick! Through this little door. It might lead somewhere."

It didn't. It was a wooden cul-de-sac, scarcely worthy of the name 'cupboard'. It was empty and gave the impression of never having stored anything, I don't know why. Then we heard the manager singing. Either he had gone completely mad or else was using an unorthodox method to lure the police inside his office. His words warbled like a wartime broadcast on an ancient radio with a loudspeaker made of corned beef.

"My bum has got a hat in, hip hip hip hip horray! My bum has got a hat in that's not coming out today . . . "

"Emerge from your hidey-hole with your hands up!" boomed a different voice.

"Look down there!" cried Fellatio.

There was a trapdoor under our feet. We had nothing to lose by lifting it up, or so we naively imagined. That's what we did. A blast of fetid lukewarm air swirled out of the hole and bathed our faces in a mist that hardened very quickly to a crust. We exchanged glances and licked our lips in an agony of indecision.

"The access hatch to the vaults," stated Fellatio.

68

"Shall we jump in or not?" I hissed.

The decision was made for us. The strident voice on the other side of the door offered no mercy. "Your time is up. Prepared to be riddled! Not with riddles but with bullets!"

I went down first and Fellatio followed. The zinging sound of projectiles demonstrated that we weren't a moment too soon. There was a large bucket directly beneath. I dropped into it and huddled down, leaving no room for Fellatio, who was forced to cling to the side. Our weight activated a hidden mechanism and we began dropping into the sticky darkness. The circle of light above diminished rapidly in size. Then eager faces peered over the rim, heads encased in mammalian helmets, those blue bonce-breasts of official brutality. The snouts of a few Tommy guns were also silhouetted, then a torch beam stabbed the black.

"Come back!" pleaded the malfunctioning megaphone.

"We prefer not to," shouted Fellatio but this defiance only made matters worse. The police were now better able to judge our current position. The Tommy guns were aimed and half a dozen triggers depressed. I'll never really understand why triggers get depressed so easily, especially in the hands of the police. If I was permanently located between a stock and a barrel I would be fairly cheerful all day. Cripes, even a soup and a flagon would be good enough for me!

The bullets whizzed past our ears, ricocheted off the sides of the bucket, struck sparks from the cable on which we depended. One even lodged itself in Fellatio's empty socket, rattling around like a simile of death. Now the faces clustered around the circular opening were obscured by smoke. Wait a minute: the ammunition used in Tommy guns is powered by cordite, a smokeless explosive, so in fact the faces were still there, clear as genital warts.

"We know exactly who you are, Mr Spit and Mr Swallow, so don't think you can escape our clutches," rasped the megaphone again. "Our clutches are overseen by the Police Complaints Commission anyway, so don't be frightened! We don't really deserve our abominable reputations. Come back up and surrender quietly to us. You can trust me. My name is Inspector Ynch Short and I work for Scrofula Yard."

"Oh no, not him," breathed Fellatio.

"Is he a bad 'un?" I whispered.

"Ynch Short of the Yard is the worst . . . "

The remainder of Fellatio's sentence was drowned out by a fresh burst of Tommy gun fire. The gloom below erupted in a cacophony of thick splashes. The guns fell silent and the megaphone began speaking again. Puzzled, I arched my eyebrows at Fellatio, who was unable to note their elevation in the poor light but who guessed the truth of my expression from the distortion in my voice: stretching facial muscles alters the timbre of speech. And talking of distortion, this is what I asked my friend:

"If the megaphone is faulty, how are we able to understand what's being said?"

To which Fellatio replied, "Ynch Short suffers from a speech impediment and the low fidelity of the megaphone circuits exactly cancels out his strange slurring."

"What an unlikely coincidence!" I exclaimed.

Fellatio probably shrugged at this, I can't be certain, but I have neglected to report what the megaphone said. Let me repair the omission! It warned us that the centipedes would be set loose if we didn't come up immediately. Ordinary police use trained dogs, but Inspector Short's men belonged to a special group that had permission to make use of unorthodox methods. Poisonous centipedes were highly capable of running down cables and inflicting painful, possibly fatal, bites on fugitives fleeing from justice in a descending bucket!

"This is your last warning!" boomed the megaphone.

"That means the multi-legged nasties have *already* been released," pointed out Fellatio grimly.

"That bastard up there is a litre short of a thimbleful of mercy," I complained.

"Not a litre, a pint," corrected Fellatio.

70

I ignored the taunt. "What shall we do? If we surrender we die. If we resist we also die."

There was no need to make a decision, for destiny or chance took charge of matters. This is how it did that. Fellatio had been hanging onto the side of the bucket with his amputation, not his real hand. Suddenly his amputation changed shape: it turned from a claw into a knife, smooth and without hooks or grips. Down he went, into darkness, before I had even finished speaking. No scream issued from his lips, only a more heroic gurgling, surprise mixed with fear.

I ought to clarify a few details about his amputation in case you've got the wrong idea. I'm sure you *have* got the wrong idea so I guess I've left it late to explain matters. All the same, better late than not at all. I'll just briefly state that a mad inventor by the name of Medardo created the *utation*, an artificial limb that regularly morphs into a variety of accessories. One moment it might be a five or six fingered hand, the next a tentacle, then a pair of tongs or a saw, then a nutcracker or bullwhip, and so on. At least a hundred different variations are available.

The earliest *utations* were clockwork and tended to run down quickly, so Medardo electrified them. This improved model was known as the amp-utation, to distinguish it from the non-electric kind. Fellatio was one of the very few people in the world who wore one[4]. The way it randomly changed shape at unexpected times had severely limited its popularity. Imagine a Swiss Army Knife with none of the functions reliable for any prolonged period of time. In fact it was worse than that because a man equipped with one of Medardo's amputations wasn't even able to choose which function would be available from one hour to the next. Not a handy device at all!

It's probably pertinent to report here that I often get Medardo mixed up with another mad inventor by the name of Mondaugen. This world of ours seems full of mad inventors! Or maybe it's just my world,

---

[4] Earlier in the story it was claimed that an unexpected sight caused his amputation 'to grow back' whereas in fact it grew *into a* back – into a cuttlefish spine to be more precise.

not yours. That's not important right now. Among other things Mondaugen created inflatable buildings for the convenience of various repressive governments and their agencies, the new headquarters of Scrofula Yard for example or the adjacent Cop Hospital. Both are fabric edifices full of pressurised helium.

I watched Fellatio fall until he vanished from sight and his jerking arms and legs were only visible because of the reflected glow of the police flashlight on the circular walls of the vault. Whoever Inspector Short had delegated for the task of aiming that stabbing beam of photons obviously had the shakes or else was a complete novice, for he consistently failed to catch either of us in his halogen rays. I looked up and perceived something hideous scuttling down the cable towards us: one of the police centipedes. At the same time I heard the viscous splash of Fellatio breaking the surface tension of the spunk reserves.

Almost without thinking I eased myself over the side of the bucket and let myself drop. This seemingly reckless action was based on sound survival principles. A bite from one of those vile arthropods would be certain to finish me off, whereas a plunge into pearly man dew, especially if my momentum was absorbed by the body of Fellatio beneath me, even from my present height, which I estimated to be about one hundred metres, could probably be repeated time and again without the risk of serious injury.

As it happens, I landed right next to my floundering comrade, splashing him mightily with the curds and whey of straights and gays. Poetry, that is. He gulped, retched, smiled, and then I wondered how I was able to see him so clearly. My eyes had adjusted to their surroundings, was that it? Only after a slurpy minute of bobbing did it occur to me that the sperm was producing its own light, a wan and eerie phosphorescence that made me curious about the inner luminosity of my own nuts. Another burst of Tommy gun fire pitted the sluggish lust ripples around us and then a merciful silence descended that gave me an instant false sense of security.

"They've given up," I gurgled in relief.

"Scrofula Yard never do that. Ynch Short is like a vulture with a beak in its beak: tenacious and ugly. He hates an unresolved case and will never shrug his shoulders over our crime and walk away. The worst is yet to come."

We waited for twenty minutes or more, while the police heads withdrew from the tiny circle of light high above. When they returned, no more shots were fired. Instead something long and thin slapped down towards us: our hose. Then a distant mechanical growling commenced and the end of the hose slurped greedily at the sloshing sperm. This sucking noise was rather unbearable and I had to position my mouth almost inside Fellatio's ear in order to be understood. Even so, I'm not sure he comprehended me.

"They want to leave us stranded at the bottom of a dry well," I wailed, "but I don't see how that will help them capture us. Better for them to shut the hatch and leave us to drown in bollock brew."

"They are using our own equipment against us," growled an indignant Fellatio. "That's really unforgivable."

The noise of the pump suddenly stopped, then resumed after a few moments but with a different kind of whine. I noticed this but was temporarily distracted by the observation that the level of the spunk in the vault hadn't gone down by so much as a single microlitre despite all the sucking. Clearly this reservoir was fed from another source. Before I could elaborate on this idea Fellatio seized my shoulder and shook me back to an awareness of a new and disturbing development in our dire predicament.

"They've reversed the polarity of the motor. The pump will no longer suck but blow . . . "

I struggled to make sense of his words. "You mean they intend to perforate us with dust from the crater in which we live?"

Fellatio shook his head. "That's not the idea, laddie me boy. They've already sucked up a thousand gallons of come. Those bastards plan to turn our hose into a bukkake cannon. Prepare yourself for the most forceful facial in history! The sperm will be driven into the pores

73

of our faces until our entire heads are saturated. It's a method of controlling riots on the sets of pornographic films."

"That's a hardcore form of dastardly!" I huffed.

"Well put, Mr Gum, I mean Mr . . . "

He never completed his sentence. But this was fortunate for me, considering what a perfectionist I am when it comes to using appropriate nomenclature in sticky situations. I could never be addressed as any kind of Spit at that point in time. The force of the hose was just too great. Warmish globules of fertile semolina eased themselves between my tightly shut lips and there was nothing I could do to prevent them slipping down my throat. I grew increasingly saturated and incensed as the white jet pummelled us in our respective mushes. The police above weren't really aiming the hose at us but leaving it to its own devices. It flapped and reared like the most mythical breed of trouser snake and scored its direct hits purely by chance.

"Another minute of this and we'll be spunklogged!" gagged Fellatio.

I felt something tugging at my leg. Thanks to the wavelets generated by our swimming motions, many of which rebounded off the walls of the vault and collided with each other, creating a complex array of eddies and minor whirlpools, we had been gently pushed to the rear of the cistern, hard against the rough back wall. The tugging increased in force. It was a current of come, probably the source that fed this reservoir. My mouth was too full of chewy fluid to explain my new idea to my friend in words. I used sign language to indicate that he should follow me, no questions asked. Despite his dreadful nature in most regards, Fellatio is a trusting soul. He never balks and rarely flunks.

I took a manly breath and dived under the orgasmic surface. I could see nothing down there, for the come burned my eyes like acid, but with my hands I felt the circumference of an outlet as wide as a blue whale's cartoid artery: big enough to take a man. I plunged through, battered by the current but grateful to be out of the far more vicious spurting of the bukkake cannon.

74

The submerged tunnel wasn't especially long, more like a gateway through a thick wall than a real passage, and with no portcullis to bar egress to the other side. I surfaced with my heart almost bursting, my eyelashes thick with a come that was already gluing my eyes shut. I tugged this gloop away in strands that resembled necklaces or beads: my eyes stung but the sight that greeted them was enough to make me shout in wonder and delight. Then Fellatio surfaced nearby and went through a similar procedure.

To say we found ourselves in a gigantic cavern would be to understate the truth. A new world with a rock ceiling is a closer approximation. In fact we appeared to be floating in an underground ocean whose waters were undiluted spunk: a sunless sea without shores or starry sky. The phosphorescence was just bright enough for me to see everything worth observing. A notable discrepancy was that we seemed to be at a much lower level than the tideline in the vault. I still haven't resolved that anomaly but there might be something in Fellatio's remark that different testicles hang at different heights on different men. Probably not.

Certainly this ocean of sperm had taken many centuries if not millennia to accumulate. Our caveman ancestors probably started it off with some hairy wanks. I hypothesise that a pair of stooping hominids called Ug and Og had a dick duel on porous soil then spurted simultaneously and so laid the first seeds, so to speak, of this titanic testicular Tethys. Who else had contributed to the seething mass in the following historical periods? It was mild fun conjuring up mental images of kings, philosophers, inventors and eunuchs beating the meat. Maybe not the last on that list. A billion horny males, a trillion wanks.

Don't question my arithmetic on that one. There are more important considerations at this frothy point. Fellatio and I were both astonished to notice that not all the come blended into a single fluid. Indeed not. Distinct currents moved through the greater ocean at a variety of depths, flowing and coiling like worried worms, many glowing a slightly different shade of white, a few even tinged green, purple or brown. As we bobbed like pubic hairs in the pale knob oil, I felt we were in a nest of living knots, a sperm shibari of astounding asymmetry. But at no juncture were we lassoed by the separate ropes of cock mustard.

We had obviously passed through a solid barrier to reach this ocean from the vault but no wall was visible. Nor was the air misty with pre-come droplets. Visibility, as I've already stated, was excellent despite the relatively low level of illumination. Wank Mutual had evidently gone to great lengths to keep this place a secret. Then it occurred to me it would probably remain a secret forever, for I was incapable of keeping myself afloat on any liquid medium longer than a few hours.

"There's only one way we can appear to have surfaced in the *middle* of this ocean," I blurted as inspiration shot its load into my mind. "There must be a gigantic mirror covering the entire side of the dividing wall."

"If that's true," sneered Fellatio, "where are our own reflections? It can't be those two solidified wavelets of crusty spunk with a vague resemblance to ourselves!"

I looked in the appropriate direction. "I guess not."

Reluctantly I abandoned my theory and didn't try to argue the point with my companion. This was unfortunate because Fellatio abruptly deflated into a mood of utter despair. Stuck in the exact centre of an onanistic ocean: what situation could possibly be more tricky or sticky? I watched his face contort with random expressions, including the ironic ones, as madness swelled like a bubonic cock inside him. There was no help for him now as he grimly surveyed the milky expanse and lashed out at it with futile blows of an amputation that had turned into a whisk.

"Please don't injure yourself . . . " I croaked.

But such considerations meant nothing to him now. The onset of extreme man-dew mania was rapid and irreversible. His real hand dipped under the self-abuse juice, fumbled with belt and buttons and suddenly he was working himself into a white frenzy. What's more with the root of *my* cock! I could do nothing to stop him. He held me off with his amputation, churning my protests into blabber batter. Faster and faster jerked his other hand. I knew what was coming, of course. Man-dew mania is invariably fatal. Trapped in a cauldron of seething ejaculate, a victim will wank himself into utter exhaustion and then drown. The frantic desire to contribute the contents of his own balls to the greater mass is a form of insanity as far beyond reason as cocks are beyond cunts. Something to that effect.

"Use a condom for fuckwit's sake!" I pleaded.

Too late. Fellatio gasped and an unctuous glob flung itself out of the writhing buttermilk and spattered him in his good eye, hanging there like a magnified amoeba trained to be an acrobat. All his energy dissipated at that exact instant. He yawned, snored, threw back his head and went under. No surfacing three times for him! I never saw him again: doubtless the bones of his skeleton are still drifting on different come currents, his flesh having been devoured one molecule at a time by those treacherous tadpoles that biologists refer to as 'conception fish'. You may be surprised, dear reader, to learn that I have hated spunk ever since.

With my business associate and best friend dead and my own demise not far off, my mood turned a trifle sour. Yet salvation jammed its own foot into the closing door of my luck only a few moments later. The greenish form of an old sailing ship loomed over the masturbation horizon. I yelled and waved at it, a foolish segment of my brain wondering if Fellatio Nelson had somehow forgotten to drown and was coming to rescue me instead. Many aspects of this ship were similar to those of Fellatio's old schooner. But there were important differences also. This vessel was larger as well as older and somewhat more imposing. It also exuded a reek of pure evil that wasn't convincingly muffled by the stench of the fuck spittle on which it rested and through which it ploughed like the ultimate advocate of sloppy seconds.

I grew afraid, very afraid, more afraid than an albino pegged to the outside of a parasol, and with my spunk-encased complexion and eyes moody and scarlet from prolonged contact with the acidic passion pus I was probably the very image of one of those pigmentless pygmies. Not that albinos are particularly short but I like the alliteration. Notwithstanding that, the ship came closer. Instead of swimming towards it, I threshed in panic in the opposite direction, my head permanently angled to gaze back at its sinister bulk. I squinted. It seemed that a different figure was front-crawling to meet it. Was it Fellatio or perhaps another poor sperm-sea castaway?

I redoubled my efforts and so did this figure. Curious. Then I collided with something very solid and the sky was no longer starless. Nor was the loin glue below me. My life didn't flash as I began to drown: it kept its clothes on and was perfectly discreet, a gentleman.

Something hard hooked the collar of my shirt: a hard hook. I'm always troubled when things are exactly what they seem. Connected not to a stump but to an exceedingly long wooden handle, that hook. Up I was hauled, spluttering like a fish cliché, onto a deck of rotting emerald planks. The face that looked down at me was featureless and utterly green. No, it was an olive in very close proximity, not a visage at all! I was being offered sustenance. I opened my mouth, clamped it shut, my teeth shearing the flesh off a stone I then spat sideways. Another was presented and I took it.

"Nothing like the tang of pickled olives to negate the taste of accidentally ingested spunk," remarked a voice.

I nodded weakly and gasped, "Fellatio . . . "

The voice chuckled. "Not for me, thanks, but I'm sure some of my sailors will take advantage of your offer later. If I had any sailors. I don't, in fact, and I crew this ship alone. An onerous task. I'm cursed, you see, but I bet you *don't* see with all that crusty come in your eyes. Having said that, you saw the reflection clearly enough."

"What do you mean?" I asked.

78

"Fooled by the giant mirror, you were," he explained, "which was erected by Wank Mutual years ago to conceal the sluice that feeds their vaults. The ship you thought you were swimming away from was a reflection of my ship and you smashed straight into it. An easy mistake to make and while we're on the subject of reflections I'd say it's no reflection on your character, whatever that might be."

I groaned in despair. "Fellatio is dead."

My rescuer shrugged. "Fashions come and go even in sex, but I'm sure the practise of oral gratification will come back. In the meantime permit me to wash the throbber custard from your peepers with the liquid in this olive jar. Clogs the tear ducts does trouser snake spew."

The vinegar in the jar burned almost as badly but my vision cleared enough for me to behold my saviour in all his *yrolg*, the exact opposite of glory. He was horribly familiar and intensely demented and I instantly knew the voyage was doomed. The flaking paint on the hull, the rolling yellow fogs, the odd habits of the captain . . . But actually the hull was coated with slime, there were no fogs and his habits were despicable rather than odd. I was remembering an earlier ill-fated journey on a ship not dissimilar to this one, a jaunt made in the company of a virginal young lady, and the force of my *déjà vu* took away all my breath and took away all my breath. I knew him but he didn't recognise me yet. The crust of spunk was an effective disguise.

"I'll soon clean that gunk off you," he said.

"Don't bother," I squirmed. "Distract me instead with some idle chatter. Who are you and what is your curse?"

He frowned and pulled his chin. "Very well. But first a brief lecture on spunk itself. The mystic man substance which coats your body and bathes my soul in the bleach of lust isn't a simple juice squeezed from the testicles, but a complex cocktail manufactured by a skilled team of glandular barmen inside the body, to wit: the prostrate gland, bulbourethral glands, pinocyotic vessels . . . "

"To wit, to woo," I muttered idly.

79

He jerked his head and fingered the hilt of a flenching cutlass at his belt. "You work for the owls? You are an agent of those feathery backgammon-playing deviants?"

"Oh no!" I cried. "I was referring to a different sort of woo, the wooing of a lady, so we're still on the subject of spunk, or at least are skirting around it . . . "

"Skirt." He rolled the word on his tongue and finally decided he was satisfied with my explanation. "Yes quite. As I was saying, nuts aren't the only contributor to the finished product, though they tend to get all the credit. Aside from bollocks, we mustn't forget the role of the Sertoli cells which nurture the spermatocytes, the Ductuli Efferentes that modify the love fluid by making it thicker, the Epidydimus that adds glycerophosphocholine to the brew to hinder premature capacitation — in other words the too early priming of those wriggly little fellahs — and the bulbospongiosus muscles that provide the necessary push to get the blighters up the urethra."

"My education has been furthered," I said gratefully.

"What more would you like to know?" he asked.

"Your name and the nature of your curse, as you've already promised. How did you end up down here?"

He rubbed wearily at his eyes. As he did so the ship turned sharply to the left. I looked over the rail and saw we had narrowly avoided a collision with the mirror wall, an incredibly expensive sheet of silvered glass that contained my shocked face among billions of cubic tonnes of reflected phallus foam. Clearly this ship was following a preordained course.

My rescuer seemed to read my thoughts. "The steering is entirely automatic and that is a condition of my doom. My name is Rip Van Wankel and this semi-phantom vessel is *The Frigging Crutchman*. I invented a new method of beating the meat and that's why the supernatural powers controlling the universe — in cahoots with a consortium of sperm bank directors — expelled me to this priapic perdition. Do you realise exactly where we are? This isn't an artificial

80

sump but an entirely natural feature. We are in one of the bollocks of the Earth itself! The left hairy kumquat to be more accurate . . . "

"You mean to say that Mother Earth is male?" I shrieked.

"She is now," replied my host in a voice of unbearable misery, clutching his own tackle in inadequate empathy.

"So the sperm banks fib about the source of their reserves?" I gasped. "What a scandal waiting to be exposed!"

"The Earth has never had sex," continued Rip Van Wankel in his most dismal voice, "and indeed has been a virgin for untold billions of years. Well not exactly 'untold', because the age of our world has been the topic of many conversations, but you know what I mean. The pressure of the planetary spunk is now so great that a discharge would be a catastrophe comparable in whiteness to the worst Ice Age but far more violent. Even the orgasmic contractions would be off the Richter Scale. Pray that our globe remains celibate, will you?"

I took him at his literal word and because I had been on my knees since he deposited me on deck it was easy enough to intone a few words of spiritual pleading. I prayed not to a deity but to myself, to the divine scribbler Mr Gum, finest of all make-believers, tutor supreme! Did I answer my own prayer? That's my own business, you insolent little snooper. Please maintain some distance between our lives. I am the Gum, you are a Sap, a considerable difference.

Rip Van Wankel sighed and kicked at a coil of rope near his feet. "Ordinary masturbation technique is very inefficient. I realised how wasteful it is from an early age. It's a piston-like motion, up and down, very linear, but only the down stroke contributes to the actual wank. The up stroke is redundant, a gap in the generation of delight. My new rotary self-abuse method, named the Wankel Wank, creates continuous pleasure by eliminating the up stroke. Men of every nation were on the verge of a new auto-erotic era but my hopes were scuppered by the powers that be."

"That be what?" I wondered.

81

Rip Van Wankel ignored my confusion and grunted, "Well now I'm down here for eternity, however long that might be, a doomed bad egg not yet hatched into a fresh myth. Something like that anyhow. And you are with me. You must tell me all about yourself, I'm sure we'll get along just fine. Are you an enthusiast of engineering? I am. I hate irrational things like magic and witchery. Can't abide vague disciplines and their so-called adepts."

I took a deep breath and said, "I was a teacher of the art of telling lies, a Creative Writing tutor, so I know how to sniff out a porky at the distance of a vastly extended metaphor. That's about half the distance from transfinite to infinite in case you're wondering. You are telling porkies now. You're not an engineer but an evil scholar of magic, the exact opposite of what you claim to be. I bet the name of your ship isn't even *The Frigging Crutchman*. You're a fraud and a . . . "

"Yes it is!" he blared. "Well not quite. Almost. I inherited this galleon from a certain Captain Dangleglum, I'm sure you don't know him, and I renamed it. That's my prerogative."

"What was it originally called?" I demanded.

He shrugged. "The *Tm-bloody-esis* or something along those lines. Why should you care?"

"We travelled together once, you and I, when I was escorting a young lady named Primula, probably better known to you as Lynne Truss, and you told me about a diabolic whistle belonging to the Knights Templar that . . . "

Rip Van Wankel suddenly sprang forward and clawed the spunk from my face, casting handfuls of the stuff in all directions, working frantically until my true visage was revealed. "So it's you! Mr Mug. I might have known!"

"Mr Gum," I corrected, politely but firmly.

"Oh yeah? Mr Mug you are to me: a right cupful of idiocy. Think I can't rattle you on board my own vessel? You'll be a *sore sir* after I've finished with you — that's a pun on the word 'saucer', a ceramic disc sometimes associated with cups."

"But never with mugs," I snorted.

"You goddam mugtree, I'll teach ya!"

"Gumtree," I corrected, impolitely but softly.

"Come here, you crummy cuppa!" he spluttered and before I knew what was happening, or to be more accurate before *you* knew what was happening, I was securely bound with the rope that had lain at his feet. Seems that Fellatio and myself weren't the only devotees of shibari in this story! He didn't gag or blindfold me, however. Not kinky.

"Are you going to torture and slaughter me?" I whimpered.

"Forfend!" he returned in a hurt tone. "Rip Van Wankel doesn't do stuff like that. Debatably he's a liar, but no brute. He intends, in the third person and elsewhere, to deposit you on an island that *The Frigging Crutchman* always passes on its endless circuit around the pearly deeps, an isle that's a convenient distance from the mouth of the cannon into which he intends to load your form."

"I'll be smashed to smithereens!" I protested.

"Not so, Mr Porcelain Drinking Vessel or whatever your name is. The island is not uninhabited. There are igloos, many of them, and bigger buildings too. I'll aim at one of those and the soft snow will absorb your inertia."

"Igloos are made of hard ice!" I roared.

"To be honest," he said sadly, "these kind are constructed from the bizarre cock cheese that accumulates under the rim of the glans in uncircumcised men and is known as 'smegma'. I didn't want to tell you that because I'm sensitive to the feelings of my prisoners."

"You've done this before?" I cried aghast.

"The prog rock keyboardist Jan Hammer was my first victim," he giggled as he rubbed his hands together.

"Liar!" I screeched. "He played fusion jazz, not prog!"

"I possess not one of his albums," yawned my tormentor, hefting me towards a cannon already packed with gunpowder. As he forced me into the barrel with a ramrod I was amazed at how this scene replayed in miniature my earlier descent into the vault of Wank Mutual, with its

83

contracting circle of light and its . . . Well in fact that was the only point of resemblance. There were no police megaphones, no centipedes, no Tommy guns.

As another aside, I was later informed by Jan Hammer himself that the reason that particular gun is so inaccurate is because all things called Tommy are deaf, dumb and blind. But they sure play a mean pinball. He told me this in a song. Not the most reliable source of factual data concerning firearms.

I enjoyed many hours of conversation with Rip Van Wankel in the hours or perhaps even days that followed. He wanted to know what I had done with his sorcerous whistle, the one that summoned bedsheets into life. I told him it had been left behind in the seventeenth paragraph of my first tale. He considered this a bit careless because any other character could re-read that passage and pick it up.

"Not so. I buried it under the words 'unbroken hymen'," I said.

"A shoddy precaution," sniffed Rip Van Wankel. "That's the first place anyone would look in a sentence!"

Fair point. But I had lost interest in the whistle long before and now desired only to get this unpleasant phase of my life over with. My wish was granted shortly after. The strike of a match, the hiss of a fuse and then immense pressure beneath my feet. I was flying through the air towards a flock of igloos, the ship behind me, but I fell short and landed on a beach of crushed tagnuts. I didn't bother to look back and wave. Already I was converting my mentality into that of a castaway. I would offer Creative Writing lessons in return for food, catamites and a high tribal rank. I intended grimly to survive.

"Look what the spunk washed up!" giggled a contemptuous voice.

I raised my head and groaned.

"Glad to renew our acquaintance!" the voice added.

I glowered at the bellicose dwarf who danced before me. "Hymen Simon no less. What a small world — with insulting emphasis on the word 'small'."

But the infinitesimal blighter didn't stop his victory samba. The first time we ever stared each other in the face was on a beach the same as this one, well not quite the same, utterly different in fact. On this shore the waves attempted to fertilise anything spherical, beachballs included, and that's not your usual kind of surf. I thought about kicking the squeaking creep in the head but he was such a tiny target I couldn't be moderately confident of making contact. Plus I was still tied up.

So then I thought about fleeing. But he was already hollering for reinforcements and instantly groups of savage and dissolute men emerged from the igloos and converged on me, most armed with clubs and spears of hardened smegma in their arms. Double plus, I was still tied up.

"I'm the chief of these exiles now," Hymen Simon chuckled.

"How did you accomplish that, you atomic homunculus?" I asked with genuine curiosity.

"They are scared of my whistle — the whistle that makes bedsheets come alive. I blow it occasionally to keep them in line — or in any other pattern I please!"

"Including pentagons?" I was sceptical.

He roared with vile laughter. "Even hypercubes if necessary, you pretentious plop! The whistle is powerful juju, dig? It makes me a big flap on the scene."

"How did you recover it?" I pleaded.

He stood with hands on hips and whistled mockingly. "Let me take you back not very far to a time when I was known as Peter the Tenant. You defrauded me of all my sperm and my girlfriend Claribell Teddyface walked out on me. Without any come I grew so depressed I committed suicide and went to meet my maker. That's who we all meet when we die. But who is *my* maker? That's right, the whistle! It blew me into life when I was just an intact maidenhead between the lower lips of young Primula."

"Logical enough," I remarked.

He acknowledged the compliment with a smirk. "So I had the whistle: all well and good. But I found I was trapped under the words 'unbroken hymen'. Was this my tombstone, I wondered? Impossible because I was actually a broken hymen. Put *that* in your plonker and choke it!"

"Yes, I will. Thank you," I said.

"There was a trapdoor beneath my feet. I opened it and found a slippery pole which I slid down with no hope of return, into the sea of spunk. The whistle was safely clenched between my teeth and I blew it, turning the fabric-like crusty surface of the stagnant ocean into a temporary face that provided instant assistance by rearing up in a giant wave, opening its mouth and blowing me — not sexually, you understand — all the way to the shores of this island before breaking up."

"A remarkable entry into the left testicle of the world," I commented.

"That's not how I did it," mumbled one of the henchmen, shifting his dormant club between shoulders. I blinked. It was Jan Hammer. I possess not one of his albums either.

"I want revenge. On you," breathed Hymen Simon.

Desperately I tried to distract him. "I wonder what's happening on the surface of the planet right now? Think about it. All those lives, all those professionals going about their business, all those hobbyists and even housewives. How strange to picture with the mind's eye the teeming billions collectively known as mankind. So many pussies being humped, babies being born, infinitives being split! Consider a location at random, a city among the mountains, for instance Salzburg or Chaud-Mellé. Imagine the things that are happening there right now! All that drama, all the comedy, the interplay of human emotions, the solidly constructed characterisation, the disappointments, hopes, mixed feelings, betrayals, badly worded sentences, romantic interludes . . . "

"You're about to pay dearly," growled Hymen Simon.

86

"What can I say to distract you?" I pleaded. "I'll say anything to make you forget about me."

"Coward!" sneered the nasty dwarf.

"Very well. *Coward!*" I roared, to no effect.

Unbeknownst to either of us, at that exact moment an astronomer in the aforementioned city of Chaud-Mellé mounted his telescope and then it up on its tripod. I have nothing against men who fuck optical apparatus they later intend to use. This astronomer's name was Batavus Droogstoppel and after he wiped his jism off the lens he peered up the skirts of the night. What he saw made him gasp and jump back in alarm. "They are on collision course! They are almost here! We are all possibly doomed!" he wailed. He thought about alerting his friends and neighbours to the danger, and by default the world, but finally decided not to. The physical act of contraption-coitus had left him feeling too tired for even the smallest amount of running out on the street while waving his arms and screaming.

"Another bloody aside?" growled Hymen Simon.

"Afraid so," I admitted.

The horrid dwarf indicated a large building that resembled a slaughterhouse. "Don't worry, it's not that," he reassured me, "but a clinic that specialises in circumcisions. I intend to lop your foreskin off!"

"But why, why, oh why?" I implored.

"Ages ago I asked you a question you never answered — don't you think it strange that a hymen can be male? The truth is that *all* hymens are male. It's a ying and yang thing, a speck of male in everything female, a speck of female in everything male. By the same token all foreskins are female, including yours. Claribell Teddyface was an animated foreskin, the perfect soul companion for an animated twat flap!"

"By all the Commas of Truss!" I cursed. "You plan to turn my foreskin into a new girlfriend for yourself?"

"One blow of my whistle after your helmet hood has been severed from the sausage proper and I'll have a replacement for Claribell! Yes, that's my fiendish plot!"

"And what will you do with her once you've got her back?" I spluttered in outrage.

"I'll fuck here twice a day and spurt my cream in her quim almost exclusively. On special occasions, such as my cock's birthday, I'll use her mouth and spray the back of her throat. Very rarely I'll wank myself off between her tits and never will I penetrate her bumhole . . ."

"In that case you're welcome to it," I said.

He was annoyed by my nonchalant attitude. "The operation will be performed without anesthetic, of course."

"Wait! Wait!" I bellowed. "Answer me one question before you do the terrible deed. Does a hymen's cock have its own foreskin that can be turned into a woman with a hymen that can be turned into a man, etc?"

"I've never looked," was the disappointing reply.

Hymen Simon then barked an order which resulted in his henchmen snatching me aloft and carrying me towards the clinic. Despite the strength in his fingers Jan Hammer had problems with my weight. The clinic doors were flung open and I was rushed into a theatre. A performance of Beckett's *Krapp's Last Tape* was just coming to an end. We crossed the stage and exited through another set of swing doors into an operating room. There was no need to strap me to a table: I was already trussed up good and proper.

The floor was littered with rings of flesh. Foreskins. Nobody ever swept up in here. Some of the older prepuces were so desiccated they crunched underfoot like hula hoops. The snack, not the game. And not under my feet.

"Down with his trousers," ordered Hymen Simon.

"One more question!" I screeched. "How is it possible for a grapevine to speak?"

"Only by whining," badly punned the dwarf. Then he raised the scalpel and lowered it. At that precise moment there was a terrible roar from outside and an incredible shaking. Foreskins rolled back and forth. Hymen Simon slipped with the scalpel and severed the rope binding me. I wriggled free and jumped up.

The henchmen were in a flap. Jan Hammer chewed his renowned knuckles in terror. "Sounds like the world's having sex and is about to come!"

"Feels like that too," I concurred as I swayed.

"Impossible!" barked Hymen Simon. "What celestial body would make itself available to fuck the Earth? No other planet fancies our own world, nor any moon or member of the asteroid belt. Even those non-discerning sluts called comets haven't hit our geophysical sack since Tunguska in 1908. Face it, the Earth's no looker and no charmer."

"There's someone for everyone and something for everything," mused Jan Hammer sentimentally.

"The Rings of Saturn are to blame," I said with sudden awareness. "They were detached by Frabjal Troose's gravity beam. They must have reached the Earth, encircling our globe like cunt lips around the swollen glans of an aroused cock. Our planet has fucked them and is about to shoot its load. We are in its left bollock. Can you guess what will follow?"

"We are about to be ejaculated?" blinked Hymen Simon.

I nodded. "Out through the cock of the Earth. Does anyone here have any idea where *that* is?"

"According to rumour, Mount St Dangly's," said Jan Hammer.

I frowned. I was on the verge of a twist ending. I felt and resented this, but didn't voice a complaint. I snatched up two loose foreskins from the floor, tied them together in a reef knot, an easy thing to do with any pair of closed loops, and grabbed Hymen Simon with my free hand, dragging him outside and down to the shore. None of his henchmen followed.

The spunk sea seethed. All manner of irrelevant thoughts passed through my horrified but fascinated mind as I beheld the sickening spectacle. Did the manager of Wank Mutual still have a hat up his bum? Which part of Mr Lavender in Club Cockring was a lady and which part a boy? Would Fellatio Nelson ever have a column erected to him rather than *at* him? Was Ug the Caveman my own ancestor? Did Lynne Truss ever irrigate her own semi-colons? What did Victorians get up to when they weren't living in their Age? All very confusing, maddening, peculiar.

Then everything went white. The money shot!

I was flying upwards, borne aloft on vertical currents of subterranean jism, mouth choking but with the dwarf still in my grasp. The pressure lessened: we had emerged from the tip of the Earth's cock! The spunk fog cleared. We were above the clouds, in a sky so dark blue that the stars were visible, and all around us the sparkling Rings of Saturn: a rather loose quim in my own opinion but clearly adequate for our world. Good job they weren't the Rings of Uranus! Something large and dark approached us. I gasped. My house! What was it doing so high in the sky?

We landed on its porch and I inserted my key into the lock. The door swung open and I pushed my prisoner onto the least comfortable sofa, twisting his hands behind his back and slipping them into the foreskins. I didn't need to turn on the television news to understand what had happened. Not that the television was working anyway. The realisation of the truth made me laugh with an aggressive mirth that communicated itself to Hymen Simon, that vile midget bitch. We roared together, without a particle of hashish between us.

Frabjal Troose had constructed his mansion in the crater of Mount St Dangly's! Fellatio and I had been living on the tip of the Earth's penis without being aware of the fact! No wonder I had never seen a volcano in the vicinity: I had been looking *outwards* for one! So much for the footprint of an asteroid: our dried out sea was actually the dimple on the end of a petrified pork sword. Mr Gum hates being wrong but in this case he was paradoxically delighted.

The house reached the highest point of its trajectory and began falling back down. The impact would surely kill us. But I didn't give in to feelings of compassion and release Hymen Simon. I wanted him to die in fetters.

"Like the fetid fucker you are," I explained.

Our velocity increased. I refused to look out the window but remained in a rocking chair opposite the sofa. It occurred to me that if I ran a bath and immersed myself in it, some absorption of shock would be achieved. But the hot tap was faulty and only produced water in a thin trickle: it would take too long to fill a bath that way and I refused to dunk myself in cold water. So I remained where I was, a rocker.

"If I'm truly a rocker," I babbled to my unwilling guest, "then you must be a mod."

"I'm a magically aware sheet of vagina skin, you shit," he responded bitterly.

"I know, just humour me."

"You ruined my relationship. I'll never be reconciled to you in any way. Your Creative Writing lessons were rubbish, incidentally."

I cuffed him across his face. There are many things beyond the pale, not just albinos. He bled from his upper lip while he smirked. Then we both fell silent, waiting to be squashed, to metamorphose into jam.

But it didn't happen that way. No siree! We landed smack bang — or hiss burp — on the roof of Scrofula Yard, that inflatable headquarters designed by Mondaugen. Remember how I mentioned him? Thought I was just going off on a tangent, didn't you? The building collapsed but neatly cushioned our plummet. We were uninjured, undisturbed in fact, which is more than I can say for the policemen who were stationed inside at the time. When the tattered fabric settled, the few survivors were rushed off to Cop Hospital, less than a hundred metres away.

One of those survivors was Inspector Ynch Short. When I went to visit him in his sickbed he was in remarkably good humour. I feared I would be forced to apologise but he waved the incident aside. I hurled Hymen Simon at the foot of his bed as a sort of gift.

"Well done!" he beamed weakly. "We've been after this ugly git ever since the President declared squeaky little fellahs illegal last year. And what a nice touch, using spare foreskins as a pair of handcuffs."

"They can also be employed as foot manacles and garrotes," I said.

"Capital! You know something, Mr Spit . . . ?"

I didn't have the heart — or the guts — to inform him of my real name. "Give me a clue."

"Ho ho! I don't know why that's funny but this paragraph's making me chuckle. Anyway, my point follows: as you are so good at arresting criminals, why not come to work for us on an official basis? Scrofula Yard is rather short of staff at the moment. He he! You can be my assistant."

"I don't know," I fidgeted.

"Come on, Mr Spit," he coaxed. "You'll be perfect for the job. Think of it this way: I'm something of a Sherlock Homo myself, so you can be my Watson. Watson Spit, that's you! Do you like it, buster? What's on, Spit?"

"Particles of food mostly, sir!" I replied naively.

"Ha ha! Villains watch out!"

I licked my lips and pondered the matter. Maybe it was high time for the excellent Mr Gum to contemplate another career change. Why not? Poachers can turn into gamekeepers. Spunk robbers can just as easily become the lackeys of famous detectives. I agreed to the proposition. We shook hands on the matter. Then we pummeled Hymen Simon between us in a weird ritual that possibly had something sexual about it. That's for you to decide, you filthy perverts.

Spermicidal Maniacs

Where the Sun Doesn't Shine

"HOPE YOU'RE READY for your first case," said Ynch Short of the Yard as I reported for work.

"Ready as I'll ever be!" I answered smartly.

"Good man, Mr Spit. Anyway, the mystery that confronts us today concerns sunbeams. I mean actual planks of sunlight. You know what I'm referring to: we've all seen them slanting through orchards and high windows."

"Plums and oriels, sir!" I confirmed briskly.

"Mind your language," he muttered, then he picked at the scabs covering his neck. His injuries had healed badly but at least he was alive and still had a career, unlike so many of his colleagues. Our new headquarters were located in a small caravan park and Inspector Short's office was one of the more battered and rusty trailers.

"What are those sunbeams up to now?" I asked.

"Well it's a terrible thing, a crying shame, verily," he sighed as yellow pus dripped down his fingers, "because they appear to have turned evil. That's the sum of it. Sunbeams once were the policeman's friend: they were *good*. They kept away night terrors and the powers of darkness. If a vampire went outdoors when sunbeams were slanting then he would burn to ash in an instant. Like a beanburger in a crematorium furnace. Oh yes!"

"Have they stopped burning?" I asked incredulously.

"Beanburgers no, vampires yes," he replied.

"But do they even exist?" I gasped.

"Vampires yes, beanburgers . . . well they're on the way out, I would say. Trends in vegetarianism."

94

I was so shocked that I sat down. Only my first morning as a police lackey and I was already parked on my buttocks. What was the occult coming to? Vampires strolling about in the day like tourists, beanburgers being given funerals like ordinary decent human beings. I briefly wondered if I was the right man for the job. This was much harder than teaching Creative Writing to no-hopers who had more free evenings than sense. But I'm no softie, that's the important thing.

"When did they change allegiance, sir?" I enquired.

"Beanburgers or vampires? Neither ever have, to my present knowledge. They barely even fluctuate."

"The sunbeams," I clarified.

His frown vanished and he consulted an open file on his desk, shuffling through papers and continually shifting the Tommy gun that served as a cumbersome bookmark. "Let's see. About five years ago, according to this."

Had I been drinking coffee I would have spluttered it all over the front of his shirt. "What! And you're only tackling the issue now? That's very lackadaisical, if you don't mind me saying so. Surely it's the job of lackeys to be lackadaisical, but you are the most famous and vicious detective in Scrofula Yard. Or have I got it all wrong, sir?"

"Badly wrong," he stated, "apart from the famous, vicious bit. Don't you realise that every police force has a vast backlog of cases to tackle? We never fight contemporary crime, with the single exception of sperm bank robberies. Five years is much less than the backlogs of other police forces. Some of those chaps are still searching for Ug the Caveman. He embezzled a mammoth, so it's said. But that doesn't concern us as much as sunbeams should. Dig?"

"Sure thing, buster," I responded.

"Let me brief you more fully," he offered, finally leaving the Tommy gun and his scabs alone. "Sunbeams stopped hurting vampires half a decade ago. In fact they began nurturing those undead suckers. There's one unborn every minute. Chap named Barnum had that to say

95

about vampires. Petey Barnum, something like that. Don't know what police force *he* worked for. Now where was I?"

"In your office, sir!" I informed him.

"What? Ah yes, thank you . . . Anyway, the stronger, thicker and more profuse the sunbeams, the happier and healthier the vampires. Doubtless you can imagine the consequences of this peculiar reversal? The vampires of the world began migrating to the most sunny locations, chiefly to deserts, where cloud cover is minimal and the sunbeams are ferocious. They thrived on the fierce ultraviolet light, becoming physically powerful and handsomely tanned."

"Is the Sahara full of them, sir?" I prompted.

He smiled smartingly. "Now it is, yes. And not just the Sahara: there are other deserts in Africa. You'd know that if you'd ever crossed the continent in a chariot pulled by trained vultures. Centipedes aren't the only creatures we work with here, my lad! The vampires have taken over the deserts. They've also stopped drinking blood, another recent development."

I rolled my eyes. "They drink sperm instead, I suppose?"

He nodded. "Your bloody puerile author: he hasn't bothered to come up with an explanation for the change! I can almost visualise him sniggering away."

"With respect, sir, he's your author too . . . "

He scowled and spat. "Worse luck! The vampires got bored in the middle of all that sand. Nothing much to do. So they started digging canals that stretch all the way to the sea. Soon the deserts were irrigated, dotted with lakes of brine. The sun evaporates that water, leaves the salt behind, sends up clouds that rain fresh water at night. The ground is saturated, agriculture becomes possible. The vampires have turned into farmers and the keepers of orchards."

"Where do they get their sperm food from?"

"Two sources. They plant spunktrees and harvest the nuts. Creamy goodness! They also entice human settlers with the promise of fertile fields and virgin forests. Then they suck off those poor saps until they're drained."

"The diabolic deviants. Let me at them!" I roared.

"Hold your centaurs, I mean horses, Mr Spit! We don't plan to send you to Africa, our budget won't allow it. We can only afford your bus fare to a maximum distance of fifteen kilometres from Scrofula Yard. The nearest true desert of any sort to our present location is found in Almeria, Spain and that's a distance of 1753 kilometres, so you won't be going there either."

I performed swift mental calculations. "From the data you have just supplied I estimate our present position to be on the site of the lost city of Wolverhampton. Nobody knows how it was lost or who lost it. Forgetting all that, where are you sending me, sir?"

"More or less," he said, twiddling his scabs.

"Did I hear you say *Moron Lust*, the quaint village between Idiot Desire and Cretin Arousal, also quaint villages?"

"No, I was referring to your speculations concerning the Hampton of Wolves. No matter! The truth is as follows: you are going to pay a little visit to the Sunbeam Research Centre midway down Solstice Street. What's more, I'm coming with you! Ynch Short never stays put when his Watson goes off. Which reminds me: please withdraw that magazine from that rack and consult it, will you?"

I did as I was bidden. The magazine was the latest edition of WHAT'S ON: DEBAUCHESTER, giving details of the times and places of every *Watson* in the locality for the coming week. I found the relevant page and learned I was scheduled for a minor adventure with a solar theme at 11:00AM, less than one hour from now. So there was no time to lose! Inspector Short was already dipping a hand into the pocket of his jacket for sufficient coinage to purchase two bus tickets.

We ran out of the station, almost tripping over the cable that connected the caravan to the electricity generator that fed the entire park, then we slowed our pace and walked three kilometres down a muddy woodland path to the site of the original Scrofula Yard. Families of the slain were burning the inventor Mondaugen in effigy, an automated effigy Mondaugen had invented and provided in a futile attempt to earn forgiveness from the victims.

To demonstrate solidarity with such hatred, Inspector Short emptied his Tommy gun at the jerking figure: he carries it everywhere. The robot deflected many bullets with its huge crackling hands but a few ripped open its charred clockwork abdomen.

The people cheered. I grinned somewhat sourly.

On the verge of Unrest Avenue we waited for a number □ -1 bus. Not a number 69, you dirty minded louts. Boarding the lumbering vehicle we took our seats upstairs: all passengers are required to bring their own stools. The journey was uneventful and quite short. We passed the notorious cathedral with its mortar of crushed bones and blood and I waved at a gargoyle. Friendly chap, I am, forthsooth.

We hopped off at the corner of Solstice Street, leaving our stools behind. We also forgot to disembark with our seats. With an uneasy feeling that toilet humour was in close proximity, we marched along the pavement, reaching the main door of the Sunbeam Research Centre a few minutes later. Inspector Short rang the bell.

"What are we doing here, sir?" I hissed anxiously.

He spoke sideways and I listened at a suitable angle. "It's like this, Mr Spit. The sunbeams must be persuaded to revert to their old ways. They must change allegiance from vampires back to humans."

"This institute doesn't control the sun!" I protested.

He shrugged. "I know that, I'm not stupid, but it's our best shot. This is the only place within our reach that studies the sun and its emissions. The people who work here must have built up a good working relationship with that fiery sky orb, a relationship based on trust and spectroscopy. If anyone can pull strings with the sun, have a word in its flaming earhole, so to speak, it's them!"

"Worth a try," I agreed despondently.

He rang the bell again and we waited for almost a minute before a hatch in the centre of the door slid back to reveal a leering mouth that said, "Yessssss?"

We were taken aback by the sibilant accent. Do all sunbeam workers talk like that? Then the mouth closed in a grin and an awkward silence prevailed. I felt agitated but did nothing. Inspector Short found the tension unbearable.

"How may we help you?" he asked the mouth.

"I beg yourrrr pardon?" came the reply.

"Do you have an appointment?" Ynch Short persisted.

"Noooo," said the mouth.

"In that case, do you agree that meetings without appointments are perfectly satisfactory?"

"Yessss I do!" hissed the voice.

"Open the door then!" commanded the Inspector. And when the scrape of a moving bolt indicated that his ruse had worked, he winked slyly at me. We stepped over the threshold into a corridor that smelled of solar flares. I frowned. The trick hadn't been so clever after all.

"We're the police and you have to do what we say anyway," I informed the owner of the leering mouth.

Then I looked more closely at him.

I wish I hadn't, because although there was nothing obviously sinister about his appearance, he gave off an aura that inclined me to shivers, or perhaps it was his bearing or maybe just the way his shadow on the wall kept moving even though his body was perfectly still, or maybe my imagination was simply working overtime, as my work contract specifies. Certainly his visage and clothes were above suspicion: a long pale face with two pointy teeth, highly arched eyebrows, black hair as slickly greased as a tango dancer's, a voluminous dark cloak with a scarlet inner lining. Quite unremarkable.

"Make yourssselvesss at home," he lisped.

"Thanks buster," I replied.

"Will you show us around?" asked Inspector Short.

Our host licked his lips while his shadow performed abstract gyrations. "Asss you wissssh. Would you care for sssssome coffee?"

"A nice cup of. Two sugars. Milk," said the Inspector.

"A mug for me," I added.

"Miiiilk?"

"What's that?" I wondered.

"Tit spunk," explained Inspector Short and I considered this interesting concept. What a truly amazing world we dwell on, a ball grimed with endless variations and possibilities, all mind positively boggling. But I declined the offer with a grimace. Some concepts are *too* interesting.

"Sssssugar?"

"Darling," I responded.

Inspector Short grew angry and fired a short burst at the ceiling. Plaster flaked like dandruff onto a head already covered in dandruff that flapped like very small handkerchiefs. "No flirting on the job, you slacker. This is *work*."

"Indeed sssssssso," the creep answered for me.

I was instantly a professional again. "Yeah, show us around and no funny business. And fetch that goddam coffee, will ya?"

"What's your name first?" barked Ynch Short.

"Doory," came the answer.

"Why so? What the divil did they mean, your folks, giving you a cognomen like that? What was that — you gave the name to yourself? Did you ever hear such a thing, Mr Spit? This dude thinks he can pull our plonkers right out!"

I reached forward and throttled 'Doory' with my strongest hand while I flicked the end of his nose with the fingers of my weakest. "You heard the chief. Spill the beans!"

"It's instant coffee, not freshly ground!" the poor fool yelped as he twisted out of my grasp. "There are no beans to spill, only granules. But we're wasting time, I'm a busy monster, I mean man, and I want to help

100

you with your enquiries as efficiently as possible, so I can get back to work. Follow me."

He stalked off down the corridor, cloak swishing, and we kept close behind, the Tommy gun trained on our host's shadow, our nostrils flared in reaction to the electromagnetic stench. The passage opened into a large circular chamber, a solar observatory that was also the centre of the building.

"Thissss isss where the work takessss place."

"So this is where you commune with the sun," the Inspector sniffed. "Nice pad you've got here."

Our host stepped towards another door with the word KITCHEN stencilled on it. I couldn't imagine what lay behind this hinged and knobbed barrier. He passed through and I exchanged wary glances with Inspector Short. The hiss of escaping steam reached our ears. "In the name of every correctly placed apostrophe, what's he doing in there?"

He emerged a minute later with a tray on which rested one cup and one mug. Inspector Short took the offered coffee, sipped thoughtfully and confided to me in a whisper, "I just don't know!"

Our host had closed the KITCHEN door tight.

"Fond of doors, aren't you?" I jabbed my mug in his direction aggressively. "Opening and closing them."

"That'ssss why I call mysssself Doory. But I operate many doorsss in the courssse of a working day, ssso my full name isss Poly Doory. Poly meanssss many. It'sss a literary reference too!"

Inspector Short ignored what was probably a cleverer-than-thou challenge, one neither of us understood. "A bloody woman's name, if you ask me. Poly put the kettle on!"

"He already has," I pointed out gingerly.

Pouting at the misunderstanding, Doory waited meekly for us to commence our investigations. I gazed around the chamber. The ceiling was transparent, a vast lens that focussed sunlight onto a crystal that stood on a pedestal in the middle of the room. Banks of consoles and monitors were everywhere. The men slumped over them were peculiarly thin and dry and rather pale. I wondered why they didn't acknowledge our presence, why they were so silent.

"Becausssse they are bussssy," explained Poly Doory.

"But they aren't even moving!" I protested. "So how can they be working? They all look fast asleep."

"I made a missssstake. They are ressssting. On their teabreak. Not busssy at all, jusssst relaxing."

"Why are all their bones exposed? What happened to their flesh? This is most irregular!"

"Not at all," insisted Doory. "The Sssssunbeam Ressssearch Centre operatesss on a very ssssmall annual budget. Cutbackssss. We can only afford to keep a ssskeleton ssstaff . . . "

It was a good answer. I was stumped for a witty retort. But Inspector Short wanted to wrap the case up quickly. He pointed to a telephone resting on a desk. "Is that a hotline to the sun? I want you to call the big yellow ball right now and ask it to stop aiding and abetting vampires."

I snarled at Doory, "Do what he says, pal. Or he'll pop a cap in your mule. Savvy, buster?"

The cloaked cretin nodded sombrely and stepped towards the desk. He could tell I wasn't bluffing: Ynch Short of the Yard would poke a fedora into a mouse if he had to, the guy was a fanatic, a real vicious copper. So we stood and watched as Doory dialled a number on the antique contraption and began lisping into the mouthpiece like a cocksucking aristocrat with a cobra wrapped around his impediment.

"Oh hello. Issss that the ssssun? Thisss isss the Sssunbeam Resssearch Centre again. I have two gentlemen here who have assssssked me to asssk you to reversssse the allegiance of your rayssss. Can you do that? You will! Excellent! Thanksssss very much. Have a good day. Byeee!"

"One moment!" I barked. "Don't put the phone down."

I stepped over to the desk, held the earpiece to my head cunts —
as I like to term my ears — listened for a few seconds, nodded and
beckoned Inspector Short over. The voice on the other end of the line
was cold, calculating, automatic, informative, wise and bleak, but it was
most definitely not the voice of Señor Sol. It was the voice of Tempus
Fuckit.

"At the first stroke the time will be eleven forty two and forty five
seconds. Pip pip pip."

"Who the hell is Tempus Fuckit anyway?" I asked.

"The man — or entity — who recorded the voices for the Talking
Clock," the Inspector told me. "He's dead now. Was arrested for gross
misconduct and vile sexual perversion outside the workplace and did
the rest of his time in the clink."

"What was his crime?" I persisted.

"He opened a shop selling toy violins for children. The name of
the shop was 'Kiddy Fiddles'. I arrested him with my own bare hands
clothed in knuckledusters."

"Good job you did. But his voice lives on."

"Aye, an example to us all — a bad example! Let's forget about
him and turn our attention back to this Doory jerk. My opinion is that
the blighter's a vampire!"

I winced. "You don't say?"

Poly Doory swished his cloak like a tempest tossed tosser, then
threw back his head and laughed. "Ssso you have guesssed my
ssssecret? Ha ha! I infiltrated thisss building five yearsss ago and perss-
suaded the sssun to join our caussse, the caussse of the undead! Then I
ssssssucked dry all the sssstaff until they became nothing more than
dessssiccated husssks with big sssmiles on their mummified facesss.
Now I'm going to sssssuck you off, ssso that my sssecret will be ssssafe
again and the vampiresss will continue to dominate and irrigate the
dessssserts of the globe!"

"Desserts?" I repeated with a frown.

"He means deserts," said Inspector Short.

"Oh those," I said.

"Watch out! He's heading for your groin. I anticipate a fatal act of fellatio, Mr Spit!"

Inspector Short's warning came a little too late. Already the vile no-gooder had my trousers around my ankles, underpants also, and was coaxing my dangly into stiffness with flicks of his tongue. The Tommy gun clattered but Doory's shadow had started running in a tight circle around our struggling forms, its incredible speed creating a black un-yielding barrier. The bullets bounced off and smashed the skeletons where they sat. Whoops! My cock began to grow.

"Call for reinforcements," I gasped.

"Sure thing, kiddo," responded the Inspector as he dashed for the phone on the desk. He dialled a number and shrilled into the mouth-piece, "Come quick! To the Sunbeam Research Centre! Trouble with a vamp! Oral sex act also!"

"I'll have ssssucked both of you to deaaaath long before your col-leaguesssss arrive," mumbled Doory.

"What did he say?" asked Inspector Short.

I shrugged. "Sorry. Didn't understand a word. My fully extended throbber is stuck halfway down his throat."

"Ssssssalty, cheessssy with a tang of nutmeg . . . "

"Hang on in there, Mr Spit! Help is arriving soon. Just keep your pecker — I mean pluck — up, don't despair! In the meantime I'll just play with the crystal on this pedestal that seems to be absorbing solar energy."

"Leave that alone!" gagged the vampire. "It'sss a very danger-oussss object. That cryssstal hasss already accumulated enough power to illuminate a fridge!"

"Nope. Still can't make head nor tail," I admitted.

"Maybe I'll do the crossword in this old abandoned newspaper in-stead," said Inspector Short. "Let's see. One down, eleven letters. Act of licking pussy not necessarily to orgasm . . . ?"

"Cunnilingusssss," suggested Doory.

"That's fifteen letters, you oaf. Plus I didn't even hear what you said," snapped the Inspector.

"When issss thissss bassssstard going to come?" choked Doory.

I began whistling a pleasant tune, at least it was pleasant to my head cunts: to the ears of anyone else it would have been an atonal dirge of the utmost annoyance. So it goes. I noticed that the vampire's shadow was growing tired or dizzy, reducing its velocity, lurching and staggering.

"No mortal can ressssist my blowjobsssss," gargled Doory.

The Inspector was still scratching his head over the intricacies of the crossword puzzle. "Eight across, eight letters. Type of hat not suitable for popping into an ass?"

"Sombrero," I answered confidently.

"I don't believe the ssssstamina of thissss man! No mortal can fail to ejaculate when I do *thisssss*."

"Yeah buster? Well it doesn't do much for me," I sniffed.

"How isss thisss posssible? All cocksss mussst come ssssooner or later!"

"Fourteen down, eight letters. The state of being without a home, also a type of cock that will never come?"

"Rootless," I said with a smile.

Doory rolled his eyes in horrified exasperation. How would he ever know that the root of my cock had been stolen weeks earlier by my former companion, Fellatio Nelson, unless I told him directly? A rootless cock never spurts, no matter how accomplished the wank or suck. I was immune to vamp's finest techniques! If he kept going for an hour, day, century or aeon, the issue would be the same: zilch!

"One born every minute," I remarked sarcastically.

He disengaged his mouth, wiped it unnecessarily on the sleeve of his cloak and jerked his head as if seeking escape routes. His shadow had collapsed and was lying prone on the floor. Then he snarled defiantly.

105

"You may have outsssssmarted me but you'll never take me prissssoner. The police are alwayssss very sssslow to ressssspond to emergency callssss. I have plenty of time to get away. Hasssta la blissster, baby!"

Inspector Short shook his head. "I didn't summon my colleagues at Scrofula Yard. I phoned the local farmers' market instead. They have hated vampires ever since the deserts of the world were transformed into bountiful orchards and gardens bursting with fruit and vegetables. Prices of such produce have collapsed over here as a consequence. Farmers are much more responsive and vengeful than policemen. They'll be here any second!"

There was a commotion at the front door of the building, a clamour of voices, the pounding of fists. Then the door shattered. Into the chamber rushed a mob of agricultural labourers wielding sickles, flails, rakes, corvos and other tools of the sowing and reaping trade. They set upon Doory without further warning, knocking out his fangs, shredding his cloak, combing his widow's peak the wrong way, dragging him back out. Robotic effigies of inventors aren't the only things that get burned in public in these parts. After the rampaging crowd had departed with their prize the chamber smelled of straw and dung.

"Better or worse than solar flares?" wondered the Inspector.

"I can't decide," I answered truthfully.

"Shall I phone the sun?" he asked.

"Do it, sir," I concurred.

He approached the hotline, lifted it off the hook but didn't dial a number. The line to the sun was direct. Sweat poured down his face. It isn't every day that a mere mortal gets a chance to chinwag with a G2 type star, not even when that star is the centre of the caller's solar system. But he remembered who he was and regained control of himself.

"If it's not too much trouble, would you mind switching the allegiance of your sunbeams back to their previous position?"

No answer. Unfriendly silence.

"Try speaking in a hissy voice," I suggested.

He tried again. "If it'sss not too much trouble, would you mind ssssswitching the allegiance of your ssssunbeams back to their previoussss posssition?"

A slight pause, then, "Yeah. Okay."

Inspector Short lowered the phone, confided in a hush that his ear was burning, that the voice he had just listened to had been half as hot as hell. "But the main thing is that it agreed to stop helping vampires. We've won!"

"Case closed," I smugly smirked.

"Come on, Mr Spit, let's get out of here. Clearly the sun only cares to communicate with things that sizzle. I don't think it's especially fond of vampires, just that the way those undead buggers speak accords with what the sun considers correct intonation. I think we deserve to celebrate our victory."

"Shall we gurgle vodka and rum, sir?"

He gave me a thoughtful look. "That's one course of action. Or we could pay a visit to Hymen Simon, that disgusting shred of porking evidence, in his dungeon, then pummel him between us in a weird ritual that possibly has something sexual about it. Just for an hour or two."

"Can we put him on the rack?" I squeaked with delight.

"Sure thing, pal. Let's go."

While we waited for the number ☐ +1 bus, he turned to face me with narrow eyes and said, "Maybe we should go back to my office first, put the files away and lock up."

"Right you are, buster," I replied.

We reached Scrofula Yard less than one hour later, feeling golden inside with our success and appearing golden in the honeyed sun of early afternoon. I didn't trip over the electric cable on the way back. We entered the battered caravan and Inspector Short began tidying his desk. Then he frowned deeply.

"There's an extra page in the vampire file that we haven't read yet. Here it is."

"Read it now, sir," I suggested.

He did so and his face fell. "Bad news, Mr Spit. The vampires have been planting trees in the fertile deserts: the shade is starting to kill them. They are depriving themselves of the sunbeams they now need to remain healthy. Had we done nothing today they all would be extinct in a month or so. By changing the allegiance of sunbeams again we have unwittingly saved those swishing demons. We have reconciled them to the darkness that is now a feature of their habitat. All our work has been wasted! In fact we've made the situation worse."

I was at a loss for words. "Oops."

"You know what this means, don't you?" the Inspector groaned.

"What sir?" I breathed.

"It's time for a cover up, laddie me boy. Watch carefully. There'll be plenty of these in the days ahead."

He was right. There were.

Cop Hospital

"**I** THINK WE should tackle a really notorious crime today," mused Ynch Short of the Yard with a grin.

"Something sick and nasty, sir?" I asked.

"Yes. Get me the Guild of Freshly Fucked Whores on the phone. You'll find their number on this business card that I happen to have in my pocket. I'll just reach in and rummage around for it. Plenty of stuff in here. Old mints in fluff. Here it is!"

He extracted the card and threw it at me. I caught it before it slashed my forehead open. Then I dialled the number. "What shall I say to them when they answer?"

"It's very simple, Mr Spit. Just demand to know why they haven't engaged the services of Scrofula Yard yet. Considering what has been happening to their members it's a disgrace they haven't bothered to contact us."

"Righto! I'll do just that!"

Inspector Short whistled tunelessly through his teeth and I couldn't tell if he was pretending not to be interested in the telephone conversation that followed or was serenading the Tommy gun on his desk. Both actions are typical of him. As it happens, the telephone conversation was pithy and one sided. As soon as the connection was made I said:

"This is Inspector Short's office, Scrofula Yard. Why haven't you alerted us yet? Know what happens to people who *don't* snitch, don't ya? You shameless hussies!"

Then I slammed the phone down.

"Nice slam!" commented the Inspector, between notes of his melody. "I didn't realise you were such a fine slammer."

"Nothing to it," I answered modestly. "I can slam doors too. Windows. Even tankards on mahogany tables."

Inspector Short beamed. "You'll go far in this organisation."

The phone rang and I snatched it up.

"Nice snatch!" commented the Inspector and I sighed.

"It's for you," I said.

"Ask who it is," he insisted. Such a meticulous man!

"The Guild of Freshly Fucked Whores," I replied, "and they want to report a series of shocking assaults on the girls who work for them. It seems that a maniac is roaming the streets doing nasty stuff to prostitutes."

"Fucking hell." Inspector Short shook his head in professional exasperation. "Why do maniacs always have to *roam*? Why can't they glide or shimmy just for once?"

"Stinking perverts!" I snarled.

"Transfer the call to me," he insisted.

Even though I'm not a receptionist I knew what to do. My chair is mounted on castors and so is the Inspector's. Using our feet to propel us along, we switched positions without even getting up. Now I sat behind his desk and he was poised behind mine. Occasionally we collide when we attempt this procedure but most calls are transferred without significant injury. There's a good hospital nearby in case things go wrong, Cop Hospital, an inflatable edifice full of liquids that pong and sting.

I busied myself with the work before me, even though I didn't understand what it was, while he growled a greeting into the mouthpiece, using a napkin to muffle his voice.

"Whaddya want, missy? Yeah maybe this is Inspector Short, maybe not. Yeah maybe Scrofula Yard ain't open for business, maybe 'tis. What's it worth to you, chickadee? Okay spill the beans, all of them, but not that one — too late! No matter. What colour are your knickers?"

"Bet she's nude under her clothes," I sniggered.

110

The Inspector ignored me and began jotting on a notepad. He squinted a professional squint, coughed an amateur cough, nodded a curt russell, which is a kind of nod. Then he slammed the phone down, mimicking my own slam, and sighed. He continued to jot.

"I have all the details now, Mr Spit. The woman I just spoke to is called Mrs Madame, real name Cynthia Sinful. She's the boss tart of the Guild of Freshly Fucked Whores, dig? She wants us to catch that molesting madman who goes and comes by the name of Rip the Jackoff. He's the maniac who has been doing all the recent roaming."

"Did you see her face?" I asked. "Was she smirking? Playing a practical joke, perhaps?"

"Nah, light don't travel down telephone wires. But I made a sketch of her probable visage and I want you to look at it and tell me if you think it's the face of a liar or not. Can you do that, Mr Spit? The contours of my drawing are based on the modulations of her voice, the way she slurred her vowels, chewed her consonants. Also based on my memories of Mrs Madame when I visited her last week to hire a prostitute for a quickie."

He hurled the notepad at me and I caught it before it impacted my groin. I studied his drawing: the crude outline of a retired front line tart who was now earning big money as a manager of fresher and less ambitious girls.

"An honest expression, guvnor," I said. "Her eyes say it all, so does her body language. I reckon she's on the level, capable of no trickery or japes. Suggests that Rip the Jackoff is real. Guess we've got work on our hands."

Inspector Short nodded slowly. "My opinion is the same as yours, Mr Spit. I guess this means we can open the letter that Rip the Jackoff sent us a month ago without fear we're wasting our time."

"Time is money," I remarked archly.

"Sure is, buster. That's why we regard the firing of a pistol at a clock as pornography — it's a money shot, you see."

"I'm so glad I work here, sir!" I cawed.

With an indulgent nod at my gratitude, he rummaged in his other pocket and pulled out a crumpled envelope. Then he reached into his boot and drew out a cruel letter opener and sliced open the papery thing.

"How did you know who it was from before it was opened?" I wondered.

The Inspector unfolded the letter and began reading, but he answered my question as soon as he had finished. "Because the wicked beast gave his name and a return address on the back of the envelope — 8 Herpussy Road, Debauchester. Thoughtful of him but I still think he's a villain. I just wish we had some clue as to his whereabouts!"

"What does the letter say, buster?" I asked.

The Inspector recited the horrid text from memory:

"I am down on freshly fucked whores and I shan't quit soldering them till I do get buckled. Grand work the last job was. I gave the lady no time to squeal. I love my work and want to start again. You will soon hear of me with my funny little games. My tool's so hot and long I want to get to work right away if I get a chance. That Mr Gum is a fucking awful writer. Good luck. Your unfriendly neighbourhood molester, Rip the Jackoff."

"That's rich coming from him," I said, not really knowing why I said that but knowing that life is full of unknown sayings and incidents, so I didn't fret too much. We clearly had a very literate and dangerous adversary, one who was a trifle archaic to boot, for nobody posts handwritten letters instead of sending emails. Not these days.

"But we're not actually on the internet, Mr Spit," I was reminded.

"Wondered why my inbox was mercifully free of spam! I don't have an inbox!" I guffawed.

"Ho ho! You're the limit, Mr Spit!"

"Yes I rather am, aren't I? But let us return our excellent attentions to the criminal outrages of Rip the Jackoff. I wonder if that monicker is a pseudonym? We need to examine some evidence, maybe interrogate

112

his victims. Incidentally I'm mildly disappointed that the Guild of Freshly Fucked Whores doesn't have an amusing acronym."

"That *Is* *Truly* *S*hameful," agreed Inspector Short.

"What's the plan, sir?" I asked.

"I approve of your idea, Mr Spit, really I do, about going to speak with some of the sluts who were on the receiving end of Rip the Jack-off's assaults. Fortunately they are presently recuperating not far from here: in Cop Hospital in fact. Let's go and visit them."

"Cop Hospital!" I exclaimed.

"Yes indeed. What's the matter with that?"

"But that's a hospital for cops, not for civilians. We can't demean the edifice in such a manner!"

"Easy now, Mr Spit, don't get your knackers in a knot. Scrofula Yard sometimes employs females as well as males: they are frequently known as 'policewomen'. More than a few of these beings work under-cover, posing as a variety of working humans, including maids, sewers, midwives, trombonists, trapeze artists, beekeepers and even whores. Trouble is, we tend to forget who is working undercover, why so and what as. Thus it's safer to offer hospital beds to all prostitutes who require medical attention. Just in case. Why are you frowning, Mr Spit?

"You said sewers, sir. Don't you mean seamstresses?"

He shook his head. "Policing's a dirty business, laddie me boy." He gazed wistfully into space and made flushing motions with his hand. "No matter. To work! To Cop Hospital! Last one there is a big hairy toe! Come on, Mr Spit, why are you lingering?"

"For the sake of the reader, sir!" I insisted.

And indeed a brief digression at this point is nothing more than an act of courtesy. Cop Hospital, you see, is the finest and most valuable asset our police force owns. When the Scrofula Yard headquarters were moved to the caravan park, Cop Hospital was moved with it, not a difficult task considering it's an inflatable building pressurised by helium or nitrous oxide, I'm not really sure which. It contains surgeons and nurses and medicines but originally it was never intended to have a fully functional role. Let me explain.

Back in those more innocent days, the chief passive form of entertainment was something called 'telly'. Nobody knew where it originally came from: a few fanatics claimed that the lollipop sucking demigod Kojakalhu invented it to keep mankind in its place. But they couldn't say where that place was. Whatever the truth of the matter, not to mention the truth of the energy, our society had an almost unbreakable addiction to 'telly', an object which was a box with a glass side that displayed dramas featuring little actors. The whole thing was powered by electricity and the little actors weren't real people. Or rather they *were* real but not as little as the size of the box would suggest.

The dramas that appeared on 'telly' were mostly poor travesties of amateurish nonsense. The lower classes preferred those shows that fell into the category of 'detergent ballets', in other words sagas that were open ended and often continued for decades or until all the regular actors died, sometimes longer. Sagas about the police were popular, rivalled only by sagas about hospitals. It was only a matter of time before someone came up with the idea of blending these two most successful formats. The man responsible for that synthesis goes by the name of Stuart Ross but he doesn't really belong in this tale, or anywhere near it, so I'll quickly move onto the next sentence. Actors were hired and the sets were constructed so that *Cop Hospital* could go on air as soon as possible. Enormous amounts of money were invested to ensure that the show was a resounding success.

Unfortunately for the producers and broadcasters, things don't always go exactly as planned in the long distance entertainment industry. Generally bland and predictable, the tastes of the lower classes can occasionally fail to be stimulated by corny pap, nobody knows why, and the ratings for the pilot show were abysmal. The masses preferred to remain loyal to traditional 'detergent ballets' such as *Unicycle Detectives* or *Underfunded Trauma Ward* or even the domestic abuse free-for-all *Corner Shop Bickering*. The official newspaper critics were hardly more positive

114

about the merits of the drama. After only six episodes it was taken off the air.

But it seemed a shame to tear down (deflate) an edifice designed by the great Mondaugen or to sack the actors hired to play doctors and nurses. After a series of hurried meetings between Scrofula Yard bigwigs and the show's producers the whole thing was sold to us at a reduced price, cock, smock and barrel[5]. At last we had our own hospital. True, the first patients tended to die in botched operations but over time the actors became genuinely skilled surgeons and anaesthetists. By the way, the biggest bigwig of all the Scrofula Yard bigwigs is Mr To Be Arranged, a hunched but shadowy figure who is also head of the Police Complaints Commission. People who detect a whiff of corruption in such an arrangement are just being cynical.

A few very paranoid fellows suspect that Mr To Be Arranged is actually an evil puppet master in disguise. I know for a fact that he's heavily involved with charity work and makes regular donations to the Impenetrable Disguise Foundation. Thus I rebuff those who wish to cast aspersions! He's a fine fellow and never explodes in a rage, or in any other way, and not just because I'm compelled by my contract to say that, bless his cordite socks!

"Finished your digression, dude?" asked Inspector Short.

"To be sure, to be sure, why the divil do you ask me such a riddle at this hour o' the morning!" I replied.

"Good stuff. Let's git movin'."

"Lookee here, shiftin' my butt is what I'm about. Right behind you, dear chap. Banzai!"

And so we strolled out of the office and capered the short distance to the main entrance of Cop Hospital. I was overawed as always, my hairstyle felt unworthy, ditto my teeth. "Oh vast and lonely edifice," I intoned, "pray prepare your bouncy portals to admit our humble forms."

---

[5] The barrel in question belongs to the Thompson M1928 submachine gun, of course.

Inspector Short was less effusive. "Aye, 'tis a nicely grand construction, a rare enough sight indeed."

And into its depths went we.

The whores had been given a ward all to themselves and it was difficult to remember that I wasn't in a brothel when I went to do the rounds with the Inspector. I didn't chat with all of them because too much whore talk tends to bewilder me but I got the full gist, if not jism, of their horrid experiences from those I did speak to. Rip the Jackoff had attacked with no word of explanation, coming out of the night like the tock of a clock, in one hand wielding a soldering iron connected to a battery pack on his back. He wanted only one thing: to fry the sperm leaking out of their freshly fucked money makers. That white liquid hissed but never screamed. Those wriggly fellahs have no mouths.

"Luv a duck, that's how it 'appened; ripped me knickers off with 'is free 'and, 'e did, not so much as a by your leave, neither. Nuffink I could say would deter 'im. In slipped 'is 'eated tool and me cream pie was vaporised!"

"Did the same thing happen to you?" I asked an alternative whore.

"That's right, me darlin', just like that it was, been fucked right good 'n' proper and lots o' the jism leaking back out; up comes this gentleman, never a word out o' 'is lips, and 'fore you knows it me knickers are off and the beautiful cream is cooked to death in a trice; singed me lips also."

"What about you?" I asked a third tart.

"Nuffink different to report, mister. You the fuzz, is ya? Was going 'ome after a gangbang; took a shortcut down a narrow alley, then this bloke jump out o' a doorway and thrusts 'is bloomin' soldering iron in my own narrow alley, genociding the spunk up there!"

"Almost as if the sperm was his real target," I mused.

"Exactly my thoughts," agreed Inspector Short.

"It was just one thought, not several, you shouldn't have used the plural. No matter. This is the kind of thing that makes me want to retire somewhere rural like Purloin My Liver or Organ in Cider."

"Why so?" wondered the Inspector.

116

"The punctuation of these girls! It's really appalling. Mrs Madame spoke the same way on the phone. Do all whores abuse the language in this manner or is it a peculiarity reserved for freshly fucked ones?"

"Those are my favourite kind: that's all I know!"

There was nothing more to be learned here. We bowed politely to the patients, had a feel or two, then departed the way we entered, breathing deeply of the wondrous formaldehyde as we passed back through the portals. Halfway to the office we both turned on our heels to survey the magnificent structure. It was sagging a little on the west wing and a few of the tethers on the other side had started to fray. I had a sudden vision of the whole thing breaking free and rising into the sky, a dirigible clinic, and drifting on the zephyrs not to where demand was most acute but wherever the isobars enticed it.

"Cop Hospital would look stupendous up there," I murmured, pointing at the clouds, "but the loss would be catastrophic."

"Cop Hospital," repeated the Inspector with a dreamy smile.

"Cop Hospital," I breathed ardently.

Then we tore our gazes away and trudged back to work. I sat behind my desk, the Inspector behind his. Five minutes passed. Then he said suddenly:

"There's only one way we'll ever catch Rip the Jackoff and that's to set a cunning trap."

"Like a deadfall?" I asked.

"More of a honey pot lure," he replied.

"Are you thinking of using a woman as bait, sir?"

"Yes. I want you to work undercover, Mr Spit. As a whore. Not any old whore but a freshly fucked one. Rip the Jackoff only goes for girls oozing spunk."

"But I'm a man," I pointed out.

"True alas. You'll have to wear a false vagina and a fake bosom. Dr Sadismus in the forensics caravan can sort you out easily enough. You'll also need to acquire other female characteristics. Do you know how to wrap your head in a towel? How about shopping for longer than one half hour?"

"I believe I can do both of those activities, but to be perfectly frank I'm not the right choice for this job."

"Nonsense. You're my best officer and *not* only because you're the only one I've got. Believe it, buster. With a vag and titties you'll do just fine."

"I'm really not sure about that, sir."

"Come on, Mr Spit, don't make me order you! Don't make me thrash your bare soles with a knobkerrie. Don't make me burn your un-published poems."

"I'll be happy to work undercover!" I shouted.

"Good man. Come on then, let's go and visit Dr Sadismus for some transgender treatment . . . "

I meekly obeyed and followed him out.

The caravan of Dr Sadismus resembled a cellar and we blundered into it with mildly waving arms, which is the only formal way to enter a basement. The stone walls were damp, encrusted with nitre, and the casks of amontillado in one corner were broached, emitting a smell of walled-up men. Sherry wouldn't do that. As for the sole occupant of this mobile crypt: he was bending over a toy violin designed for a child. I don't know why I found this sight so disturbing but I was glad when he straightened up and kicked the offending instrument into a dusty flock of old cobwebs.

"Visitors!" he chortled. "What can I do for you?"

Inspector Short jerked a thumb at me. "Turn him into a female, doctor, if you would."

"A female doctor? That will take years!"

"You're ignoring my commas again. Just make my lackey resemble a convincing tart, will ya? Slap on a big pair of melons, a workable quim and a wiggle, the usual stuff. I want him to be an object of desire to bearded drunks."

"Sure I can do that, just persuade him to lie quietly on this table for an hour. He looks nervous. He also looks familiar. I'm sure I took Creative Writing lessons from him at one time. New to this job, is he?"

"First time undercover," confirmed the Inspector, "but not the first time as an easy lay."

"Wears his fuckface on his sleeve," tutted Dr Sadismus.

"Now what the hell does *that* mean?" I fumed, hating to be side-lined in my own story, then I growled, "Just get it over with. Try not to make the operation hurt too much."

"Operation? That's not what we do here. We use trained fungi to achieve the transformation. That's right: mushrooms. Centipedes and vultures aren't the only lifeforms Scrofula Yard employs in its remorseless fight against evil!"

"Well spoken, doctor," approved Inspector Short.

"You mean that I stuff a brassiere with toadstools to give the illusion of breasts? That's all well and good but what about my cunt?"

"Ho ho! Your lackey's a right little tease!" joked Dr Sadismus.

"That he is." Inspector Short sounded almost proud. "But get on with it, please."

And so I was compelled to undress and recline on an uneven tabletop where the following strange procedure took place: spores were sprinkled on my groin and chest and some kind of lens focussed over these zones in turn while a secret scientific ray flooded the spores with accelerated growth energy, or some such twaddle, until they quickly germinated and grew bulbous, taking on the forms of pussy and zeppelins. I don't know what light that ray was made of, but it wasn't ultra-violet, which kills fungus, so it was probably the opposite kind, ultra-puce maybe. Ask Dr Sadismus.

They helped me to my feet and I stood there feeling more emotional and weepy than ever before, and far more unreasonable, then I remembered that I was a woman. Then I remembered that if I was a woman, I was no longer allowed to be a misogynist, so everything became alright again. Wanted babies though. I tried a few steps. Does my bum look big in this? I was naked so the answer was: yes! Suddenly I was repulsed by juvenile jokes, probably because I was by modern consensus congenitally more mature than the male of the species. I had a head, I needed a towel.

Inspector Short and Dr Sadismus walked slowly around me, whistling appreciatively and pinching my behind, then they paused to confer in whispers, but I overheard what they said:

"I swear, a guy has to have rocks in his head the size of Gibraltar to work undercover."

"Yeah, doctor, but he's not a guy now: he's a gal!"

I grew bored, lonely and ashamed standing there like that and I despairingly cried, "Isn't anyone going to give me something to cover my modesty? My own clothes no longer fit me and are no longer fashionable enough. My femininity is freezing!"

"Follow me to the costumes caravan," said Inspector Short.

We waved farewell to the doctor and I prepared myself for a long nude trek, so I was surprised when the Inspector led me back to his office. He cleared aside a pyramid of Tommy guns to reveal a wardrobe which he opened with his letter opener. The interior was stuffed with frocks and other girly stuff. His own trailer was the official costumes caravan! When I put this question to him, he blushed at the word 'official'. I didn't press the point. He offered to help dress me and I considered it impolite and subversive to refuse.

Forty minutes later I was clad in the smallest conceivable top and skirt. I also wore fishnet stockings and suspenders and high heels. There was lipstick on my mouth and a flower in my hair.

The Inspector offered me a pair of tweezers.

"To pluck my eyebrows with?" I innocently asked.

"Nope, and don't use them on your pubes, neither. Thrust it between the lips of your pussy and grip your cock with it, then work that sausage until it spews. The come should trickle nicely out of your quim. No way Rip the Jackoff will be able to resist such a temptation!

Keep it nice and creamy down there with regular wanks — but don't overdo it!"

"One small problem, sir!"

"What? Christ in a nightie: your cock doesn't have a root, you gambled it away! I'd completely forgotten about that! You're incapable of coming. Must think of an alternative plan. Luckily I prepared one earlier."

He took me by the hand and led me out of his office and we waited on the edge of Thruster Avenue for a number $2\pi r$ bus to trundle us to the docklands. Debauchester is nowhere near the sea and its jetties and cranes all seem rather forlorn, but the docklands are colourful, teeming with randy old salts and horny young peppers and vinegars for whom the term 'balsamic' is neither balmy nor barmy enough. We disembarked near a tavern called the *Dead Man's Vest* and pushed through the swing doors into a smoky space full of beer fumes, cigar ash, the clicking of billiard balls, sawdust swirls, geckos on walls, concertina wheezing and other lowlife props, both audio and visual.

"The barman is a certain Mr Vomit," the Inspector informed me, "and he's well known for his tolerance of what takes place on his premises, so just relax, take a scat and do what comes unnaturally. I'll be sitting on this other table, so call me if you require assistance."

"With respect, sir, why am I here?"

"We need to get spunk inside you, Mr Spit. These bearded drunks are our best hope. Good luck. Catch that bastard, savvy?"

"I suppose so, buster," I answered gloomily.

Within a few minutes a stranger approached and engaged me in dialogue. He said, "Nice evening, miss. You look pretty. Open for business, are ye? Here's ten euros for a quickie."

I opened my mouth to reply and suddenly it was full of throbber. Then I was lifted into the air and deposited onto the billiard table. Before I could recover my composure I was flat on my back, knickers around my ankles, brassiere unhooked and the rough hairy cock sunk to

121

its hilt in my fungoidal fanny[6]. My grotesque assailant humped one hundred times, emptied himself with a grunt, rolled off and panted. But his place was immediately taken by another, who also thrust a crumpled ten euro banknote into my hand before porking me. I saw that a queue had formed, rather a civilised sight in a den of iniquity, where the simple courtesies of life are usually forsaken. But I wasn't cheered.

The barman did nothing to stop this outrage. The apathy of Mr Vomit will always make me sick. The gangbang proceeded and I lost count of my ravishers. Even the concertina players wanted a poke!

"Inspector! Inspector!" I wailed. "I need your help!"

I saw his face looming in front of mine but my relief was short lived. The treacherous scoundrel had joined the rape! What's more, he didn't even pay me, explaining that this fuck was covered by my wages. The cheapskate! He made a strange expression as he orgasmed and something about his twisted leer was oddly familiar, evocative of the fuckface of a person I once knew. But this was no time for nostalgia: it was an occasion for dismay! I wriggled free and climbed off the billiard table, scattering banknotes like expensive skinflakes.

"You crummy vermin!" I bellowed. "How dare you rape a helpless woman in a work of fiction? All these events are made up — they don't *have* to be gratuitous. You demean the suffering of real people out there with your glibness!"

And I pointed directly out of the page.

The Inspector lowered his eyes and pulled up his trousers. His lower lip was trembling with self hatred. He made an easy target and I didn't spare him. "That goes double for you!" I spat.

Then I ran weeping into the street.

Nobody followed me but the concertinas didn't resume their wheezing. I clattered in my heels down a succession of alleys while infrequent lanterns flung my miserable shadow onto the sagging walls of crumbling houses. I stopped for a rest in one tiny square with a broken

---

[6] American readers should be aware that in Britain the word 'fanny' refers not to the ass but to the beaver.

bench and a toppled stone fountain. A trickle of gravel issued from the spout, an occasional pebble spat forth and rolled under the bench. I said it was a stone fountain, didn't I?

I let the tears flow until the inside of my head felt dry, then I grew scared. I was alone and the light was fading fast. A solitary policewoman is a tempting target for revenge attacks by the criminal fraternity. Any moment I might be zonked into concussion and amnesia by a cudgel. What a disaster it would be to forget my memoirs before I had written them! I was in a precarious position, so I decided to write them immediately: before dusk obscured my vision.

But I had no pen, no ink, no paper! There were no suitable writing materials in the vicinity. What could I do? I felt the cooling man milk leaking out of my vagina. Why not scribe my life's story with the cream of lust? I could squat and squirt the words directly onto the flat smooth paving slabs beneath my feet.

I began this mighty work. I wrote a title, 'Some Gums Do Have Them', then decided it was inadequate, so I started again. 'Fantastic Gum Mastic'. No, that was even worse! How about 'Can You Hear the Gums, Fernando?'? Absolutely wrong: I knew nobody by that name, nor they me. Slipping in wasted spunk I tried a fourth time. A book of memoirs without a memorable title is a pointless thing. 'Happiness is a Warm Gum'. Yes, by Jove, that was the one! Now I could proceed to the first chapter.

A dark figure appeared from nowhere and stood before me. It bent forward and stabbed a soldering iron into my pussy, frying my quim quink[7] and also cooking my birth canal. Soon the tiny square smelled like a cheap Italian restaurant.

"Mushrooms!" hissed my assailant. "I'm allergic to fungus! Take it away!"

The figure collapsed to the ground as a flock of rashes and herd of sniffles invaded its health and I reached out and snatched off its hood.

---

[7] A strongly alkaline ink that contains isopropyl alcohol.

"Rip Van Wankel, the inventor of the rotary self-abuse technique! So *you* are the notorious Rip the Jackoff!"

"My secret is out," sobbed the deviant. "Yes, it's true. I invented a new method of beating the meat and that's why the supernatural powers controlling the universe condemned me to eternally wander the streets at night attacking freshly fucked whores and killing sperm . . . "

"Wait a moment!" I protested. "The real Rip Van Wankel was eternally condemned to sail the sperm seas in the Earth's left testicle. And *he* was a fraud too! So who are you really?"

Then I ripped his mask off with both hands.

A head made of fruit glared back at me. "An Arcimboldo man!" I squealed. "This is too farfetched. It must be a disguise!"

And this second mask also came off.

"Claribell Teddyface! You living foreskin: I'll soon settle your circumcised hash!"

I began throttling the bitch and continued doing so for almost a minute before I remembered that a girl made out of a foreskin would be too small to hold a soldering iron. So I pulled at her face instead un-til the third mask was completely shredded.

"Lynne Truss!" I screeched.

I knew in the depths of my soul that there were no more masks. I was flabbergasted. I was in love, I was in hate, I was in-between. She crouched before me like a were-panda in heat.

"Lynne Truss! Or should I say 'Primula'? Don't you recognise me? I'm the pompous ugly idiot who took you on that boat voyage and sold you to a brothel in the very first story of this sequence!"

"No, I don't recall you. Never seen you before."

"The pompous ugly *smelly* idiot?"

"Sorry, still doesn't ring any bells."

"The pompous ugly smelly idiot — without talent!"

"Ah, Mr Mug! I mean Mr Gum!"

"Mr Spit now, or Miss Spit maybe. How have you been keeping? How are the apostrophes?"

"Up in the air mostly. Daft little fellahs. What have you been up to? Anything interesting?"

"A little of this, a little of that. Learned a few shibari knots. Became a robber. Dabbled with a bit of metafiction. It's mighty nice to see you again!"

"Likewise. I guess you'll want to arrest me now?"

"Oh Lynne, Lynne!" I babbled. "Whatever made you do such wicked things? To slaughter all that innocent sperm! Why, why, O why, buster?"

"Don't you know?" she sneered. "Didn't you hear the way those whores employed punctuation? The position of the semi-colons! As far as I'm concerned I did the world a service by preventing those illiterates from breeding more badly educated children!"

I absorbed this information with a smirk. "I have to confess that I share most of your beliefs, Lynne, I really do; I always have."

"I guess you're going to beat me on charges of premeditated spermicide?"

"Heavens no! I merely intend to caution you for appearing as a character in an obscene story. You're free to go, Lynne, I love you."

"How will you tie up the loose ends?"

"With a cover up. It's what we do best. Highly trained in such matters, we are. Off you go now and be careful. There are a lot of bloody perverts out there. Give my regards to your commas. Bye!"

Plums and Oriels

"THIS IS THE most serious case the police have ever had to deal with," muttered Ynch Short of the Yard.

"Give it to me, sir!" I begged half heartedly.

"Of course: it's yours. But first tell me what you know about prog rock. Do the names Emerson, Lake and Palmer mean anything to you? What about Van der Graaf and his Generator? Or Genesis, Yes, Camel and Gentle Giant? Ever heard of Jan Hammer?"

"I think he's more fusion jazz, sir."

"Okay, Mr Spit, this is the situation — for every successful prog rock act there are one hundred unsuccessful prog bands, such as Satori with Stuart Ross on bass. Good chaps though. I've recently done a count of all the truly successful prog rock bands and guess what? There are exactly one hundred of them."

I blinked. "Meaning?"

"Well you tell me, Mr Spit, goddamit!"

I did the maths in my skull. "There are precisely ten thousand un-successful prog rock bands in existence?"

"Yes. But also: there is one, I repeat *one*, truly monstrous ultra-successful prog band somewhere at large on this planet of ours."

"I wonder who that might be? Surely not Jethro Tull!"

Inspector Short shook his head slowly. "Maybe they've only just formed, Mr Spit. Maybe they're going to play their very first gig to-night."

And he flung at me the latest edition of PROG'S ON: DE-BAUCHESTER which I managed to intercept before it shattered my left elbow.

126

I scanned the listing until I spotted the name. "The Indigo Stripes? And Vermilion Sands is their frontman!"

"That's right. Mr Vermilion with Indigo Stripes . . . "

"I'll check them out tonight, sir, but what crimes do you suspect them of committing?"

The Inspector began playing a selection of imaginary instruments, contorting his face into bizarre but appropriate expressions. "The essential thing about prog rock, Mr Spit, is that it's beautiful — the most beautiful music in creation. That's not just my opinion but secretly the opinion of every man in existence. Some of the blighters just won't admit it! When I think of all the radical time changes on 'Tales from Topographic Oceans' and similar concept albums, my knees go weak with delight and I ask myself *how* could any bunch of humans make anything so grand?"

"Is that a Yes album, sir?"

He closed his eyes in ecstasy. "Double with a gatefold sleeve. Only four tracks, each about twenty minutes long. Cover art by Roger Dean."

I shuffled my feet. "But prog rock isn't a real crime, is it? What am I required to do?"

"I haven't finished my explanation, Mr Spit. If ordinary prog is so beautiful that it can curl the eyelashes of a science fiction reader — and it can, I assure you — then imagine what the greatest prog tune of all time might do: a tune performed by the ultimate prog rock band, in other words performed *tonight*."

"Might it cause a gentleman to shoot his load, sir?"

He slammed his fist on the desk. "Exactly! The sheer complex beauty of the interlocking melodies, polyrhythmic drumming, spacey effects and uncountable key changes will precipitate a total catastrophic draining of every working bollock on the surface of the planet, a universal orgasm so intense that the damage will be irreversible. In other words, all the human spunk in existence will be spilled at the same instant and every male body will be permanently too exhausted to manufacture new cream ever again!"

127

"Arid knackers!" I cursed.

"Yes, Mr Spit, the situation is extremely serious! The spunk will spurt until none is left, then it will cool and die! When the very last spermatozoon has succumbed, the wriggly fellahs will be extinct! No more conception fish ever again! Utter eradication of sperm life! Total planetary spermicide!"

"So many exclamation marks!" I marvelled.

"Do you prefer question marks?" the Inspector asked.

"Sometimes: I'm fond of colons too."

The Inspector raised a hand to play a really big prog chord on his invisible keyboard. I watched him closely for a few minutes as his fingers flew up and down, his left hand doing twiddly stuff with non-existent buttons.

"With respect, sir, that's fusion jazz!"

He ignored me and carried on playing, then abruptly he stopped, swivelled his chair around and propelled it on its castors to a box in the corner. Throwing back the lid, he reached inside for some items of cloth and brought them back to me. I frowned at them.

"You'll be working undercover again, Mr Spit. A prog rock fan. This is your disguise."

I studied the garments. "Corduroy trousers and a trenchcoat."

"From my own private collection, Mr Spit. Or maybe from yours. Take good care of them, will you? Here's a Tommy gun as well. Your mission is to assassinate all the members of The Indigo Stripes, including Mr Vermilion, while they are on stage. Do it *before* they reach the end of their set. They only plan to play one song. It's called 'Plums and Oriels' and comes from *Plums and Oriels*, their first album. This is the PLUMS AND ORIELS tour. It's the only song they have but it's six hours long. Don't fail me, boyo!"

"You can count on me, dude."

"Can I really? That's awfully thoughtful, Mr Spit. One, two, three . . . one googolplex . . . one googolplex and one . . . "

"I go to save spermkind!" I intoned.

"Yeah, buster, but you need to buy a ticket first. You can't just walk into a concert hall without a ticket. The ticket comes first, laddie me boy."

I scratched my head. "Do you mind if I ask you something, sir?"

"Go ahead. I'm magnanimous."

"I once had a companion — more of a sodomiser really — who used to address me in that fashion. *Laddie me boy*, he used to say, just like that. Nobody else has ever said that to me. I don't suppose there's any chance that you are really him, are you? In disguise, I mean?"

"Ho ho ho! Ha ha ha!"

"Well are you, sir? Are you Fellatio Nelson?"

"Your old buddy and business associate? Get out of here Mr Gum, I mean Mr Spit! For that to be the case I would have had to survive drowning in the sperm sea after we descended into the vaults of Wank Mutual. The whole idea is grossly implausible."

"You're right. Sorry I mentioned it, sir."

"There's no way my amputation could have transformed into an aqualung, keeping me alive on the spunkbed, until I was ejaculated from Mount St Dangly's. Ludicrous to suggest I landed safely on the Scrofula Yard building before Mr Gum did. Even more absurd to maintain that I then took revenge on the real Ynch Short by killing him. The only way for me to cover up *that* crime was to disguise myself as the Inspector and act exactly like him for the rest of my life and career — with a little help from the Impenetrable Disguise Foundation."

"Yes it's ridiculous, I apologise again, sir."

"We'll say no more about it. Run along and secure a ticket for the gig, laddie me boy!"

"Won't you be coming along, sir?"

"Love to but I'm washing my cock tonight. Do it once a month with particular attention to the root."

"Be gentle, sir. Washing's a risky operation!"

"Don't I know it. Off you go now."

I went. The corduroy trousers chafed my inner thighs. I liked it. I decided to stroll directly to the venue and obtain a ticket at the door even though the show wasn't due to start until the evening. The name of the concert hall was *The Gates of Delirium*. Very tasteful and no split infinitives: what a relief! It was a long walk from the caravan park: the hour of apocalypse for all sperm was now an hour closer. Then the dome of the concert hall loomed into view. I'm fond of domes that loom. It fills me with the expectation that they plan to weave a nice scarf or jumper in the near future. Don't tell me it's not that kind of loom, I'm not listening.

The main entrance to *The Gates of Delirium* seemed sensible enough. I approached the ticket booth where a booth-dweller lurked and I rapped on the glass with my knuckles, even though rap and prog don't mix, and I asked in a very clear voice:

"One for the show tonight, please."

"No can do, pal."

"Eh? A ticket for my good self for the musical entertainment that will take place here when the sun is abed, is what I asked for."

"None left, buddy."

"How can this be?" I fretted. "The day is still young. Prog rock simply can't be so popular in Debauchester. In the Hampton of Wolves, that legendary megalopolis, such a situation might feasibly occur. But here, by no means!"

"All the same, the gig's sold out. Not a single seat left in the place. Not bad for a debut."

"My good man, I don't require a seat. I will be happy to stand for the duration of the performance."

"Stand at a prog gig? Are you a lunatic?"

"Not at all. I am a complex fellow, part satirical, part ambiguous, who contrives to simultaneously mock and feed the clichés and tropes of modern popular culture. I'm something of a 'concept album' myself, you might say. My knowledge of prog is truly tremendous. For instance, I know that Jeff Jones was the original vocalist and bassist for Rush,

130

preceding Geddy Lee. There *are* occasions when I forget the difference between prog and the 'Canterbury Sound' but I always quickly remember that electric pianos and whimsicality are more important in the latter style of music than the former."

"You seem a paladin of prog!"

"Verily. Observe my corduroys for conclusive proof. But it goes much further than that. I played in a prog band when I was younger and we borrowed heavily from groups almost nobody has ever heard of, I don't just mean Gilgamesh and Gryphon and Egg, but Moongarden and Alphataurus and The Tangent. I'm sure you are now impressed enough to issue me some sort of special pass . . . "

"No such passes exist. All the tickets have been sold."

My voice betrayed my exasperation. "But tonight's band are completely new. Just who the hell are The Indigo Stripes anyway? And who is Vermilion Sands?"

The booth-dweller chuckled amid the booth shadows like a pneumatic puppet powered by laughing gas. "Mr Vermilion is the pseudonym of a certain Mr Lavender who used to sing in Club Cockring in Stiffy-on-Tickle. He plays bass and xylophone as well as sings."

"Good grief, what a cunning name change!"

"Quite so. As for the other members of the band: on keyboards there's The Postmodern Mariner; then we have Canon Alberic on woodwind and brass; and Lynne the Truss has the drumming duties, uses her punctuation marks to mark time, you see."

"Lynne Truss!" I exclaimed.

"You aren't listening, chico. I said Lynne *the* Truss. She's a sort of robot replica of the original woman, lots of nice cogs inside, I betcha!"

"This is really quite remarkable. I am overcome. But let me reveal a secret so sacred to the credo of prog that not even Supertramp or Marillion were aware of it, and Aphrodite's Child only suspected its general outlines. In other words it's a *hardcore* prog secret. Here it is — in their free time prog rockers like to impale little pieces of bell pepper and pineapple on cocktail sticks, maybe a few pickled onions. They are

131

snack preparers, highly proficient and dedicated! Will you let me in now?"

The booth-keeper yawned. "I knew all that already. Kindly fuck yourself away."

"Bah! A pox on your counterpoints! By the wingèd cheeses of Memirir, you are a crummy churl. I go off without fucking myself, you fuckwit, in rather a major huff. Oh yes I do!"

And that's how I went, no lie.

But I hadn't gone further than twenty-three steps before I was stopped by a shifty fellow in a long raincoat that spread out on the ground around him like a cheap cloth pond. The fish in this pond were the used green tissues stuffed into innumerable inner pockets just below the surface. My shoes ploughed the fabric waves like barges crewed by toes. He croaked:

"You want a ticket? I'm a tout, am I not?"

"I don't know; are you?"

"Aren't you aware that the President had declared touts to be perfectly legal but hasn't changed his mind about the illegality of squeaky little fellahs?"

"That's good to know, O tout-man," I said.

"Is it really? Is it truly?"

"Not especially."

"Well now," he muttered, throwing open his coat to reveal a lining that was full of shelves holding all manner of contraband. "What may I interest you in, bossman? You want some juice, fresh juice? You want a smoke of the weed? You want to visit the monkey park? I'll give you a good price, bossman, for dis is da Smilin' Coast."

"With respect," quoted I, "that is the patter of a Gambian bumster. We are in Debauchester."

"Och aye, laddie, to be sure. What the divil was I thinking of? What are you looking for exactly? A ticket for tonight's gig?"

"That's the ticket, buster — the ticket I don't have!"

132

"It'll cost you dearly, dearie. One thousand smackeroos. That's eighty-three euros in today's money. Ask anyone if you don't believe me: ask Castor Jenkins or a character from any other cycle of absurdist stories. You want a receipt? No refunds are permitted."

"I'm happy with those terms. Here's the cash!"

"Well I'd like to help you, bossman, really I would, but all the tickets are sold, every one. They were snapped up by a cartel consisting of three individuals."

"Don't you mean a syndicate of three individuals?"

"Yeah, guess I do, but it won't help you much, pal. If I was you I'd blow me own brains out with a shotgun, easier that way. I know that sentence was inappropriate but I've been itching to use it all day."

"Why is your face bathed in perpetual shadow, my good man? Just like the booth-keeper's. *Immersed* in shadow."

"Washday for features. Shadows scrub better and more mysterious than soap."

I was forced to accept the shadowy logic of this. I went away and pondered. If I couldn't attend the gig by legitimate means then I was prepared to employ guile and manipulation. I needed a disguise. The very best disguise is none at all: think of the thousands of people who never recognise you when you walk the streets of a city you've never visited before. That's because you're naturally disguised as yourself!

The gig didn't begin until sunset and the present time was only one hour after noon, so it was pointless trying to trick my way inside now. Far too suspicious an action. I decided to kill the remainder of the afternoon. But how? Luckily there was an ego sauna just around the corner. I went inside for a long session. As I sometimes do.

An ordinary steam sauna just revitalises the body but an ego sauna massages the ego, which is much better, don't you agree? You wander around a room full of mirrors and those mirrors speak to you, saying things like "you look mighty fine today" or "you're just so wonderful" or "I believe in love at first sight, I do!" I think they are powered by clockwork. Or steam. Possibly leftover steam from the ordinary saunas: that would make sense.

Maybe the mirrors were faulty when I went in or maybe it just wasn't my day, because the only response I could get out of those looking-glasses when I poked my visage into their silvery depths was, "not bad for a first attempt!"

Nonetheless I didn't flee. I'm a stickler.

When I emerged I neither felt better nor worse. That's not much of an improvement over feeling better *and* worse, but I like to take what I'm offered, so I went out with a cheerful enough face, apart from the frown and grimace. Back to the concert hall strolled I. Straight past the booth-dweller and into the lobby.

A powerful man with a shadowy face blocked my path and bunched his fists. "I'm the doorman. Where's your ticket?"

I rolled my eyes and lisped, "How can I possibly have a ticket if they've all been sold?"

"No ticket, no getting in, comprende?"

"Nein, mein herr, for I'm not your average civilian prog rock fan but a *reviewer*. That's write, I mean right, I'm the music critic for a renowned national newspaper only available locally — or is it a renowned local newspaper only available nationally? These alibis are *so* difficult to get straight, aren't they? Let me through, chickadee."

"No press was invited to the gig," he maintained.

"Come now, honeypot, I'm freelance don't you understand — my lance is always free. There may be something in it for you. The largesse of *Blue Rinse Gossiper* is legendary, partly because that paper doesn't exist."

"I have instructions to decimate anyone attempting to cross this line," he growled[8].

I raised an eyebrow. "What line, fruitful?"

---

[8] Like so many other people, the doorman misunderstood the meaning of the word 'decimate', which means to destroy only one tenth of a thing.

He slapped me across the nose, rupturing something high inside and spraying a perfectly straight line in foaming red on the green carpet before me. "*That* line, pal!"

I retreated, muttering angrily. "Keep your pesky line for all I care. Whose line is it anyway? Snot worth bothering about!"

Then I turned and ran weeping to the nearest telephone kiosk. I dialled a number but it was a long time before Inspector Short answered. I could hardly hear him over the crackling.

"There's static on the line, sir!"

"No, I think it's rustling, Mr Spit. My end, probably."

"I told you not to wash it too hard!"

"You misunderstand, Mr Spit. I'm in the very act of taking bribes and the crisp banknotes that are changing hands keep furling and un-furling, dig? Tell me your news, if you have any. The assassination is going ahead as planned, I trust? Or have you run into difficulties?"

"Just so," I answered, "buster."

"What seems to be the trouble, Mr Spit?"

I told him. He replied, "Did you notice anything odd about the three people who had faces bathed in shadows of an almost supernatural origin?"

"No," I said truthfully.

"What I want you to do next is easy, Mr Spit. I want you to *use your own initiative*. That's an order, chump, so don't let me down. It's imperative for the future of the entire human race that you get inside the concert hall and kill the performers. I know you think you're a bigshot in the world of prog but you're nothing compared to me — I once employed Darryl Way's perspex violin as a small skylight in a windowless attic — so don't let overconfidence be your downfall. Just pump those progites full of lead!"

"For the sake of all spermkind!" I roared.

He hung up. I was on my own. Then I had an idea, as was inevitable at this point in the story, I'm not exaggerating: I've passed this way before many times — Juncture of the Tale, it's called — and it's always

135

the same. Either I get an idea and something happens or else I don't get an idea and nothing happens. Or I get an idea and nothing happens. Or I don't get an idea and something happens. Reliable as tockwork, that sequence of events. Regular as a prune filled bum[9].

I checked my watch, or watched my cheque, I always get those actions muddled, and saw I had only ten minutes left before the commencement of the performance. I made my way around the concert hall to the rear entrance. I'm a backdoor man. Nobody opposed me as I sauntered through. A long and winding corridor didn't lead to your heart but to a dressing room painted green. Clearly it was envious of some other rooms. The musicians were lounging on sofas, fiddling with their instruments, sipping beverages.

"Hey my friends! Are you ready to prog and roll? I said are you *ready* to prog and . . . "

"Who the hell are you?" sneered Vermilion Sands.

"Your lead guitarist, of course, who else? I'm ready to prog and roll, yes, yes, O yes!"

"We don't have a guitarist, lead or otherwise," patiently explained The Postmodern Mariner, "because prog bands often don't need them, and we certainly don't. But you do seem familiar. Did I ever take Creative Writing lessons from you?"

"No sir, I'm your guitarist, a member of the group, stop playing silly games, pulling my leg, comrades!"

"What's your name?" boomed Canon Alberic.

"Mr Mugmguumggmuugm," I said.

"Bit of a mouthful," commented Lynne the Truss. "I think you made that up just now."

To distract attention from my blush at being so cleverly caught out, I roared, "Never mistrust Miss Truss! Looking delightfully robotic today, I note."

---

[9] American readers should be aware that a bum is actually an ass, not a tramp.

136

"Nah, I'm not truly a robot, not a sentient one at any rate, more of a waldo really: that's a kind of exoskeleton operated by a diminutive passenger. Take a look and see for yourself."

And before I could say anything in reply, Lynne the Truss raised her skirt. She wore no knickers beneath. Her cunt was a living creature, a hideous dwarf I recognised as Hymen Simon, and it was operating a series of levers that made the exoskeleton move. I was shocked and disappointed at this ghastly amalgamation of cold steel and deceitful flesh.

"Back where I belong!" chortled the pussy imp.

"How the hell did you get out of prison? I swallowed the key with my own gullet!" I roared.

"Easy. I opened the door with a bribe."

"That damned Inspector Short has betrayed me!"

Hymen Simon pressed a button and Lynne the Truss shook her head. "No he didn't. I wouldn't dream of bribing *him*. I went to a higher authority and passed a bundle of notes to Mr To Be Arranged. He can arrange anything. The Inspector can barely arrange his own hairstyle."

"Hang about!" I cried. "You can't possibly be the real Hymen Simon — I personally stretched that burst maidenhead on a rack until it became a normal sized man. He's no longer a quim dwarf, which means you're a fake! I reckon that *you* are the robot and the exoskeleton is the living thing. Am I right, Lynne the Truss?"

"Yeah, guess you are," came the crestfallen reply.

"Let's get ready to prog and roll!" I shouted.

"No way," bluntly opined Mr Vermilion. "There's no room for a guitarist in The Indigo Stripes."

"That's truly great news," I responded, "because I don't happen to be a guitarist after all. My instrument is the Tommy gun, as used in the rock opera by The Who. So what are we waiting for? Let's get out there and slaughter you, I mean them! Prog and roll!"

"Plums and oriels," corrected The Postmodern Mariner.

"Very well, Mr Mugmguumggmuugm," said Vermilion Sands after a period of accidental deliberation, "you're one of us now, one of the band."

"By all the Hammers of Jan!" I guffawed. "By all the Grapevines of Gaye! By all the Strikethroughs of The!"

"Let's go!" they roared together.

Out of the room we ran and up a flight of stairs that emerged at the back of the stage. We took our places on the polished wooden boards and then suddenly the giant curtains swished open to reveal the auditorium. Three people sat in the front row. The remainder of the concert hall was empty.

"Not much of an audience," I grumbled.

"What does that matter?" thundered Canon Alberic. "Do you think Gentle Giant cared about having any listeners when they made their *In a Glass House* album? The beauty of the music is all that matters."

"Quality is preferable to quantity," added Lynne the Truss, "but when it comes to prog the difference between the two is scarcely noticeable."

"And those three down there are very important fans," pointed out The Postmodern Mariner.

"Really? Who are they?" I demanded.

Even as I asked the question, the trio of audience members lowered their portable shadows and revealed their faces to my scrutiny. Medardo, Mondaugen and Frabjal Troose: three of the maddest inventors in the history of madness! What were they doing here? I guessed the answer at once. They actually *wanted* all the sperm in the world to be fatally unloaded from the bollocks of mankind. They were spermicidal maniacs on the grandest imaginable scale. They had bought up all the tickets to prevent an assassin gaining admittance!

Then I realised that these three wicked personalities were identical with the devious scallywags who had frustrated my attempts to enter the concert hall earlier. Medardo was the booth-keeper; Mondaugen,

138

the tout; Frabjal Troose, the doorman. But why were they hellbent on total Spermageddon? Was it because they so craved the title of 'ultimate mad inventor' that they planned to forestall any future generation producing an even madder inventor by making the production of future generations an impossibility?

Yup, that was it. Had to be. Certes.

But that still left the question: who was the maddest of the three? Who indeed!

Before I could devote another paragraph to the wicked trinity, the band launched into the opening chords of 'Plums and Oriels'. I was swept along with the music like a bookmarker in a fast paced novel. Or maybe faster than that, some sort of scramjet engine. Maybe. The melody was gorgeous, the delicate harmonies like cobwebs on the moon, the percussion crisp and evocative. I was enraptured. I stood there with my Tommy gun pointing at the floor and my mouth agape, too touched in my soul to kill anyone.

The suite progressed. That's what prog tunes do. Tend to. The very air began to shimmer, I felt light headed, happier than any ego sauna might hope to make me, and curiously this ecstasy was egoless, like an egg without a yolk or a sneeze without a nose, kind of. 'Plums and Oriels' was certainly the finest musical masterpiece ever composed in the entire history of the universe: I knew that much already. It was twice as original as 'Larks' Tongues in Aspic', 28 times more beautiful than 'The Lamb Lies Down on Broadway', 496 times more stupendous than 'Brain Salad Surgery' and approximately 6,218,032 times more accomplished than 'Script for a Jester's Tear'. Oh yes. Very nice.

The minutes went by. The notes slid past. On them.

I was entranced, paralysed, but I had to do something. The passing of time confused me, I didn't know if the song was nearly over or still only at the beginning. My ears throbbed with delicious sonic soul-food. My grip tightened on my Tommy gun. How could I slaughter my fellow band members with any sort of conscience, clear or otherwise? Surely it would be more ethical to fire a burst at Medardo, Mondaugen and

Troose in the front row? But that wouldn't prevent the abrupt emptying of every human testicle in existence. I found that I was at a loss.

I hesitated between the two sets of targets. Then I closed my eyes and pulled the trigger. I don't know where the bullets went. The clatter of the gun ceased and I opened my eyes. The stage was deserted and so was the auditorium. Where the musicians had stood now gleamed four pools of rapidly cooling spunk. I frowned. Even at the spot where Lynne the Truss had stood? That was a surprise! I jumped down from the stage, the reverberation of my weapon still echoing in my brain, and examined the seats where the mad inventors had sat. Pools of spunk shimmered on the floor beneath them.

I went outside. Night had fallen but a peculiar phosphorescence made all things visible. Torrents of spunk swirled down the gutters: the roads were rivers of the white man-milk. What kind of nightmarish bukkakeworld had I entered? It was my own world, of course, horribly altered. In the distance I spied a vast lake of spunk bubbling softly, almost a sea of the stuff. Then on the horizon appeared the crest of a fast approaching tidal wave of sperm, a spunk tsunami that was fifty metres high or more. My life was over if I didn't take evasive action immediately.

Rushing into the car park that served the concert hall, I noticed that the musicians had all arrived using their own transport. Here was the glider of Vermilion Sands, equipped with silver iodide nozzles for cloud trimming purposes; the motorised hyphen of Lynne the Truss; the turbocharged camel of Canon Alberic. And there, a little way beyond, was the small schooner of The Postmodern Mariner. I decided to requisition that for my own needs.

I jumped inside and lashed myself to the mast. Not a moment too soon! The tsunami crashed down and lifted the boat up. I heard the wet crumbling of smashed buildings, saw the concert hall collapse. The velocity of my vessel increased tremendously, scudded along like a molecule of mutant ejaculate. We were heading in the direction of Scrofula Yard. Around me the bodies of drowned people rose and fell in the frothy come. All testicles had been drained forevermore. I had failed in my mission, failed utterly!

At last the amplitude of the wank wave began to decrease and sailing conditions improved to the point where a raising of the sails would be possible, but I wasn't given a chance to do that. Something very hard knocked against the hull and a face loomed over the starboard rail. Then it said glumly:

"Nothing floats my boat — because I use a submarine!"

"Good evening, Inspector," I replied.

"You've let us all down, betrayed the world and the future of the human species, and worse than that you've been deceiving me, Mr Spit, or should I say Mr Gum — yes I know your real name. Your contemptible lies have thoroughly depressed me, I don't even care to rape paedophiles now, not that I have any spunk left to fill them with!"

"Your bollocks will make more," I insisted.

"Oh no they won't, you periodontitis of the psyche, quite the opposite — 'Plums and Oriels' has caused to be spilt *all* the spunk that will ever exist in spacetime, including every drop from the future. And it's entirely your fault!"

"I didn't compose the melody!" I protested.

He shifted his stance and I saw that he really was standing in the open hatch of the conning tower of Scrofula Yard's emergency clockwork submarine.

"Perhaps not, Mr Gum, but your firing of the Tommy gun produced the universal orgasm. You see, the tune of 'Plums and Oriels' was actually imperfect, unable by itself to force every man to spurt. It so happens that you made it perfect with the rat-a-tat-tat[10] at precisely the instant you delivered it. Those bullets were the missing notes required to activate Spermageddon. The orgasms of those in the vicinity were so intense that their bodies vaporised. You survived only because your cock has no root!"

---

[10] If you are an Italian Futurist the sound will be *zang tumb tumb* instead of rat-a-tat-tat.

I hung my head in shame. "I'm truly sorry, dear Fellatio, I mean Inspector Short, but there's nothing I can do to reverse the situation. I imagine you'll be wanting to lethally punish me with torture?"

He sighed and blinked weary eyes. "As a matter of fact, no. The bigwigs of Scrofula Yard have all survived and currently reside in the iron belly of this escape vessel. We have been holding meetings. There's only one way to save mankind. Not all the sperm will cool and die — some of it can be saved, a hand-picked roomful of the stuff, and that's where you come in."

"Really?" I blinked. "How?"

"We want you to return to the teaching of Creative Writing, to give classes to a lecture theatre full of come. Turn those spermatozoons into writers, Mr Gum! Writers mistakenly believe they are special, that they are somehow important to the world. A writer's will to live is thus greater than it should be. Teach that spunk, Mr Gum! Nurture the egos of those wriggly fellahs, encourage them to become deluded megalomaniacs — in other words transform them into *writers*! Keep alive at least a few hundred gallons of spunk to safeguard the future! Do this and all will be forgiven!"

"All?" I blurted with trembling lips.

"Some," he corrected.

And that's how I went back to my original profession. The following week I turned up to give my first lecture. The audience seethed and glooped. Here was the cream of bollockdom, each fistful of sticky man dew carefully selected from the greater mass outside, extracted from the vast white oceans that now covered the planet. Beyond these walls, less fortunate spunk was dead or dying. I surveyed the palpitating yoghurt of life and I cleared my throat. Then I began the most important lecture of my career.

"Show, don't tell," I said.

Gum, Set and Match

The Glue of the Scream

H ELLO OUT THERE! You're the reader, are you? I was told to expect you. Ought to introduce myself at this point, to create a rapid bond of empathy between us. My name is Vasily Spermcake and I'm a giant mutant spermatozoon. Pleased to meet you.

You've probably heard of my mentor — Mr Gum. I owe everything to him. But he wasn't the one who asked me to keep this journal. That was the Nobel Prize Committee. Do it for the sake of posterity, they said. So here it is! Do you like it?

I 'VE NEVER KEPT a journal before and I hardly know what to say. Maybe I'll begin with my birth. I never knew my mother, I'm not even aware of whether she was a left or right testicle. Millions of my brothers swam together in the bollock-womb and we were happy there. But there was a deep unfulfilled need within us, an unspecified yearning for change.

I remember hearing music, a complex melody with many shifts of key underpinned by polyrhythmic drumming, and I listened to it with an innocent fascination. Suddenly there was a seismic convulsion and I felt myself rushing up a narrow tube at great speed. I couldn't imagine what connection there was between this upheaval and the music but I felt sure there had to be one.

M Y BEST FRIEND at the time was Max Mayonnaise and he always seemed to know more than me about any situation. Where he got his information from remains a mystery.

Maybe his tail doubled up as a radio antenna, allowing him to pick up broadcasts from outside. I don't know.

He swam up to me and said, "An ejaculation is taking place. Pray it's a fuck, not a wank. If it's a wank we're fucked!"

TURNED OUT IT was a wank. We emerged from the tube and landed with a splat on the inside of a pair of cotton underpants. I slid off and continued sliding down a leg to the ground. It was cold there and I shivered violently. I never saw Max again.

I WATCHED MY brothers die all around me and the landscape was something from the worst nightmare. Billions of spermatozoons were dying in vast pools under a dark sky. It resembled a scene from the most disturbing dreams of Bosch. Not the human painter, Hieronymus Bosch, but Bosch Quimflake, my second best friend, also dead now, alas!

I imagined that soon I would also be dead. I didn't have the strength to wriggle or even scream. Now I would never discover the nature of my unfulfilled destiny! My predicament was excruciating. But salvation was surprisingly close at hand, for I abruptly felt myself scooped up with a tiny spoon and deposited into a test tube and rushed off by a motorcycle courier to the nearest university.

The test tube was inverted and its contents emptied into a seething roomful of come and that's where I first made the acquaintance of Mr Gum. A voice addressed the class and I looked up and there he was, standing in front of a blackboard with a delightfully pompous expression on his face. I regarded him from that moment as my surrogate father.

OVER THE FOLLOWING weeks I learned many things from Mr Gum that filled me with an increasing sense of self worth. I learned about punctuation, taking particular care over the correct use of semi-colons; I learned to shun puns and to write only from experience; I learned that a reader must always identify with the main character of a story. Other things. Mr Gum was a veritable sage, generous with his wisdom, unstinting with his criticisms.

I derived an inner strength from my attempts at writing my first short stories. I had something important to say, and that something was about me, for me, by me. My ego steadily expanded. A will to live gathered force in me: I decided to write a long novel, the longest ever written. "That takes spunk," Mr Gum remarked and he winked at me in an avuncular way. He never winked at any spermatozoon in a saucy way. Not to my knowledge.

MY SHORT STORIES were published in magazines. Reader response was extremely positive. I was hailed as *the* rising star of all genres of literature by microscopic organisms. Vasily Spermcake achieved instant cult success. I was heralded as a Dickens without the 'ens', whatever that means. Mr Gum was very proud. He served as my spokesman whenever I was interviewed and somehow he became my agent. I didn't notice the transition.

The title of my big novel was *Come Again?* and it was both a serious and ironic treatment of life in a sperm community in the backwaters of an unnamed testicle. I can't say it was precisely autobiographical. It contained a political dimension and a philosophical one. Max Mayonnaise and Bosch Quimflake both appeared in cameo roles. The twist in the story is that the chief protagonist is a *female* spermatozoon. Clever, huh? Her name is Jisma.

THE CONCEPT OF female sperm wasn't original to me. Mr Gum confessed that he fantasised about such a substance all the time. In a recess of his bedroom he had constructed a shrine to a deity called 'Vinega Stroke', apparently the patron goddess of all female sperm. He often prayed to her for the return of the root of his cock, but I don't think she had it. Certainly he didn't get it. That's how faith is tested. Also with oscilloscopes.

MY CLASSMATES DIED one by one, for they were less naturally gifted than me, until I was finally the sole remaining student in the classroom. Utter conviction in my own importance kept me going. Something else happened. It wasn't only my soul that grew but my body too. It swelled in proportion until it was no longer invisible to the naked eye. I grew bigger and bigger, eventually attaining a length of three metres, with straightened tail.

No biologist has ever been able to adequately explain how this happened. But I'm grateful it did. It made me more imposing, gave me a sense of gravitas, created more photo opportunities. My visage, such as it was, began to appear on the covers of the magazines in which chapters of *Come Again?* were published. I became instantly recognisable.

Locomotion was still a problem, of course. I have no legs. But Mr Gum came to my rescue as always: he reminded me that I was a spermatozoon and that the world was a cunt. Ergo, we were made for each other.

WHAT THAT BLESSED gentleman did was as follows: he constructed a machine to carry me wherever I wanted to go. It resembled a pram or small wagon but there was a capstan around which I could wrap my tail. When I yanked my tail and turned the capstan, a flywheel underneath the vehicle began spinning. I was able to engage this flywheel with a system of gears connected to the rear axle. Thus was I propelled along. Steering was accomplished by leaning to the left or the right. There were no brakes.

Mr Gum and I took our regular promenade every evening down the most fashionable streets of the city. People often came up to request my autograph. I can't hold a pen, so Mr Gum always signed for me. These fans also would try to engage me in conversation but because I have no vocal chords I had to rely on Mr Gum again. He spoke for me and I never once disagreed with anything he said. What a terrific fellow! Truly he was the finest agent, tutor and comrade a spermatozoon might ever hope for.

THE ONLY FANS I had problems with were those who insisted on giving me their own manuscripts to read. I was always polite at first but eventually grew annoyed at this imposition. Mr Gum did the dirty job of telling these upstarts where they might shove their unpublished works. I was grateful to him for that. And it wasn't only amateur writers who were the culprits. When the Nobel Prize Committee began hinting that the next Nobel Prize for Literature might be awarded to a certain Vasily Spermcake, I was suddenly deluged by requests from established authors.

"I would dearly welcome and cherish your opinion," said Martin Amis as he passed me the first draft of his new novel. Other famous scribblers who followed his example included Kyril Bonfiglioli, Robert Tressell, Blaise Cendrars, Germaine Greer, Malcolm Lowry, Penelope Lively, Flann O'Brien, Felipe Alfau, Stanley Weinbaum and Cormac McCarthy. Oh yes, and a chap who looked like an Arcimboldo painting with *bacon* instead of fruit for features who called himself 'Vibration Javelin'. Something like that.

THE QUEEN WROTE me a pleasant email in which she announced her intention to knight me for my services to the culture of her tottering but still viable empire. I was delighted to accept. I have no shoulders for a sword to touch — an essential part of the knighthood process — and so I designated Mr Gum as my proxy. I also suggested that he be genuinely knighted at the same time. The Queen agreed to do this, bless her.

That was at a time when the royal family were suffering from relentless attacks in the popular press for their enormous budget at the taxpayers' expense. Queen Isabel Dos had finally expired and been entombed in the foundations of London Bridge and her successor, Queen Diana the Impacted, was not yet the beloved figure she eventually became. The knighting ceremony was therefore of incalculable importance to *them*. They wanted to win back the hearts and minds of the people. Or if not the people then at least the literary crowd.

I WATCHED THE entire ceremony on an invention called 'telly', a machine possibly created by a mythical being known as Savalas the Sucker whom I didn't believe in. Mr Gum strode down the hallway, the red carpet honoured by his feet all the way. He approached the throne with the least craven attitude anyone has ever possessed in the history of the cosmos. Something that Gregory Monkeybasher, my third best friend during my youth, once said came flooding back: "The gums of the world underpin the smile of creation." No idea what it means. Gregory was a tosser.

I returned my wandering attention to the spectacle on the flickering box. Some sort of bizarre footman was making an announcement through a paper megaphone. I listened carefully to the words: "Queen Diana the Impacted, ruler of all the Englands, Jersey, Sark, the Parisian system of Underpasses, Gibraltar, Canada, Belize, Bermuda, Lower Bo, Finlandia, the House of Fraser, Zipangu, Pennsylvania, the Hebrides, Tasmania, Lipsaria, Montenegro, South Africa, the Dark Side of the Moon, Atom Heart Mother, Highway 61 Revisited, Huggy Bear, etc, wishes to make it known that the following knighthood is the greatest ever awarded to any mortal since the founding of the royal family in the year 1,608,891 BC. Therefore a sword of pure gold will be used for the touching of the shoulders and Mr Gum will be allowed to keep this weapon and melt it down for his own fiscal purposes."

149

A CHAPTER FROM *Come Again?* was read aloud by a trembling Queen Diana the Impacted and then she knighted Mr Gum. The crowd burst into spontaneous applause. But the Queen was so nervous that she made a strange and amusing mistake. Instead of saying "Arise Sir Gum" she actually said "Arise Sir Quim!" It was a shocking moment. But Mr Gum shrugged and swaggered, indicating with hand gestures that he was perfectly happy with this title. The crowd burst into spontaneous applause.

Sure enough, when he returned home and checked his (my) emails he discovered that the Nobel Prize Committee had indeed decided that the prize should go to me. Two aeroplane tickets had been booked for us to fly to Stockholm the following day. So we decided to pack our suitcases there and then and get an early night.

I N MY DREAMS I stood in the centre of a forest glade while Max Mayonnaise, Bosch Quimflake and Gregory Monkeybasher danced around me, chanting. I gathered that this was a wedding ritual. But who was to be my bride? Mr Gum, perhaps? No, it wasn't he, but a woman, not a real woman: a goddess. Yes, it was Vinega Stroke who stood with my tail between her legs. I can't say it was a wet dream — those are invariably fatal for a spermatozoon. It was more of a mystical vision. The priest who conducted the ritual was Lieutenant Colonel Jim Channon, author of *The First Earth Battalion Operations Manual*, but I don't suppose you've ever heard of him. Look him up on the internet if you feel you must.

I AWOKE IN a dry sweat, a very uncomfortable oxymoron, and I was disappointed that my wonderful dream hadn't refreshed me. Mr Gum was already up and prancing about in high spirits. We took a jalopy to the aerodrome and boarded an enormous biplane. There was room for 18 passengers but we were the only occupants of the craft. Apart from the pilots and staff, that is. Futuristic luxury. As the mahogany propellers began spinning, turning the rising sun into a stroboscope of hope, Mr Gum puffed his cheeks and remarked, "Isn't it good to be alive in *this* century! Hey, what is our century, by the way? I seem to have forgotten!"

I was unable to provide an answer due to the limitations of my historical knowledge and also because I have no mouth. So he summoned a flight attendant and asked her the same question. She adjusted her suspender belt and replied, "Well that depends on the isobars, sir. Time is now linked to air pressure. The President outlawed linear chronology last year — or was it next year? Ha ha! Do you like my tits, buster?"

"Verily I do. Stupendous melons, thou whore!" thoughtfully commented Mr Gum.

The hugely advanced flight from England to Sweden took only three days with just twelve midair refuelling sessions. I spent most of the voyage staring out of the window, hoping to spot the lost continent of Cimmeria. I failed bitterly in this task. But barbarism will outlive civilisation, I'm sure of that. Mr Gum paced up and down the aisle talking to himself or to an imaginary character called 'Fel Nel', I couldn't understand a word of it. Then he began arguing with the three people the book is dedicated to — not *my* book but *this* book — and I think he gave as good as he got. I hope so.

WHAT IS SPERM other than the adhesive that keeps life stuck to the backdrop of the cosmos? That proposition was Mr Gum's and it formed the basis for his argument with Brian Willis, Hannah Lawson and Huw Rees. They disagreed with him and wouldn't accept that without the glue of the orgasmic scream we would all have to be crucified with nails to remain joined to spacetime.

WE LANDED IN Stockholm and were greeted by Björn Ulvaeus who led us to a hovercraft and conveyed us the remainder of the distance to the Halls of Nobel. "Are you sure you intend to accept the prize?" he asked.

"Of course," answered Mr Gum on my behalf.

"Well if you change your mind I'm the first in line. Mamma mia!" said Björn.

"Keep your eyes on the road, your hands upon the gyroscopic controls," returned Mr Gum.

"Sure thing, bossman! You want some juice, fresh juice? You want a smoke of the weed? Lookee here, it's our destination already! How the divil did it do that? To be sure, there's a fine mystery! Och aye the noo, I hope you'll have a grand time!"

"We will," coldly asserted Mr Gum.

VASILY SPERMCAKE IS the new Nobel laureate. He has won the prize for Literature. His name joins the ranks of such illustrious authors as Selma Lagerlöf, Frans Eemil Sillanpää and Vicente Aleixandre. All hail Vasily! All hail Mr Gum, who made this all possible! I noticed the jealous faces of other writers in the audience. The re-condensed form of Lynne (the) Truss was there. Tim Lebbon also. Music was played over the public address system to celebrate my achievement. Prog rock. I think it was Satori with Stuart Ross on bass. Then it switched to Jan Hammer. He's more fusion jazz but I didn't lodge a complaint. Vasily Spermcake rah rah rah! The gathered people ate little cubes of cheese that had been impaled on little sticks together with pieces of bell pepper, pickled onions and olives. Prog and roll!

THEN EVERYTHING WENT wrong. The Nobel Prize spokesmen announced that my prize wasn't going to be the standard large sum of money. No, they had arranged an alternative gift, something that would guarantee the continued survival of the human race. What could it be? Curtains swished open to reveal an enormous egg resting on a vast cushion, a human egg, the egg of a woman who had accidentally expanded by a factor of several thousand after an argument with her husband.

152

"What is the meaning of this?" blurted Mr Gum as he attempted to hide me behind his back, but my wagon was seized and pushed towards the egg by the eager hands of the event organisers. To repeated calls of "Fertilise her! Get stuck in!" I was accelerated into the side of the monstrous thing. But I didn't penetrate it as a spermatozoon should. I rebounded and fell apart.

Shocked gasps filled the room. "He isn't a real wriggly fellah but a pillow attached to a length of string! We have been deceived: Mr Gum is a fraud and liar and Vasily Spermcake doesn't exist! Mr Gum wrote his book for him! Suddenly we realise it's a rubbish novel after all!"

M R GUM FLED from the hall in tears. He ordered Björn to take him to the airport but when they arrived the last biplane had just left for England. It was chugging through the sky as fast as a runaway cow. Velocity! Mr Gum was distraught but Björn had a solution:

"So you missed that double winged sucker? Big deal, sweetheart. You can enter the matter transmitter here and arrive inside a cubicle in the fuselage in a flash. No problem, hombre!"

Mr Gum nodded and followed this suggestion. It would have been equally possible to use the matter transmitter to beam himself all the way to England instantly, thus avoiding the three day flight, but such a solution wasn't stylish enough. Nope.

I N THE WAKE of the revelation that I wasn't real and that Mr Gum had created me and written all my works, it was quickly understood that my prose was awful. The Nobel Prize was revoked and the knighthood cancelled and *Come Again?* discussed in the most disparaging terms on one of those telly arts shows. Lynne (the) Truss criticised its punctuation while Germaine Greer repeatedly referred to it as 'childish', 'puerile' and 'sixth form'. This latter term bewildered me. Sixth form? As far as I was aware there were only five forms: solid, liquid, gas, plasma and imaginary. What were the properties of this hypothetical sixth form? I yearned to know the truth.

My speculations on the matter were interrupted when a sudden fight broke out between Greer and Truss. They fell to the floor in a flurry of bitchslaps, tearing each other's clothing. The host of the show, a certain Mark Lawson, jumped in to separate them and restore order but it was plain to see that his cock slipped in the various exposed orifices of those renowned and seriously taken ladies. I was forced to switch the telly off in astounded disgust.

MR GUM SQUATS in a corner of his room and rocks endlessly back and forth. The electricity and water supplies have been cut off and soon his house will be repossessed. Even though he is writing this now, for he really was me all along, he's too depressed to generate a twist ending that will restore his former glory and must resign himself to remaining stuck in an exceptionally bleak and downbeat ending.

Sticky White Hands

"YOU DON'T KNOW what you're talking about!" These words were uttered in a whine so high-pitched that the beer glasses hung in racks to dry behind the bar started to hum. The speaker was a short podgy individual with a bald head and soft scarlet cheeks. His unhealthy eyes bulged behind little round glasses and he jabbed a clumsy cigarette he had rolled himself.

The barman retained his composure and said, "I was only pointing out that from the viewpoint of science—"

"Science is wrong! Science is reductionist: that's why it's wrong! I've proved it's wrong because I say so. It's reductionist! You don't know what you're talking about!" wailed the podgy man. Opaque spittle like rancid dog's milk flecked his blubbery lips.

"—the Earth goes round the sun, not the other way around," finished the barman in a reasonable voice.

"Science is reductionist, I say! And that proves it's wrong! I know what I'm talking about, but you don't! Nobody else does! I am Samuel Tweed, the writer of mystical horror! Don't you know who you are talking to? I am the only one who knows what he's talking about! The sun goes round the Earth and there are such things as souls! I can prove it! Science says they don't exist, but science is reductionist and thus wrong! Souls must therefore exist! And my soul is eternal!"

"Well, there are many factors to consider before—"

"Factors? That's the sort of rubbish they teach in schools these days! Yes, in schools! When I was at school there was a teacher from Burma who attacked me and beat me up! And all because he didn't know what he was talking about! I hate foreigners and immigrants! I am

155

Samuel Tweed! Factors are reductionist. Schools are reductionist. They don't know what they are talking about. I am precious!"

The cheeks of the podgy man grew redder and redder as he delivered this peculiar rant. The barman wondered if he should physically eject him from the pub; it seemed the wisest course of action, if only for the sake of the integrity of his eardrums. But first he glanced around in the hope of spotting another customer he could serve, as a distraction. There was no one, the pub was completely empty.

He sighed. In that case there was nothing for it but to seize the idiot by the collar of his frayed fogey jacket and kick his pasty bloated form off the premises into the gutter where the other rats scurried. As he wiped his hands on a cloth and prepared to vault over the bar to implement this task, the door of the pub opened with a creak and another figure entered, a man in a long raincoat who walked with a stiff lurching gait like a hunchback but wasn't one. The barman squinted.

The newcomer stopped next to Samuel Tweed.

"What a retrocausal afternoon out there, it will be! The serendipity of the noumena is aesthetic!" he intoned.

"Glad you made it," said Sam. "I was beginning to think I might have to conduct the ritual on my own." He patted his bulging pocket. "I have it here, safely wrapped in tissue paper. A big custard cream in the shape of *his* face. Baked especially for me by a fool who didn't know what he was talking about, yet he baked it anyway."

"Serendipity indeed!" approved the newcomer.

"Bakers are reductionist! Biscuits are reductionist! Maybe even holism is reductionist! I am Samuel Tweed, I have a soul, a real soul; and the best writer of mystical horror ever conceived is me! Anyone who says I'm not doesn't know what they're talking about!"

"Retrocausal? Blimey, not half!"

"You tell them, Mr Weggs. You tell 'em!"

"All retrocausal serendipity of the nemonymous noumena is aesthetic, I do declare. Blimey!" came the reply.

156

The barman realised that drastic action was called for and he fumbled under the counter for the four-foot cudgel of oak tipped with iron that he frequently brandished to discourage troublemakers. During long years of working in THE TALL STORY he had become expert at cracking the skulls of idiots; the oddest customers seemed attracted to his pub. Just before he could put it to use, there was a distraction.

One of the small windows in the furthest corner of the tavern creaked upwards and a grotesque figure began pushing himself through it. As the barman watched, the intruder got stuck halfway, undulating in the style of an injured tapeworm; it was like witnessing the birth of the offspring of a pencil and a toilet, for the newcomer was simultaneously thin and fat. But surely that was a logical impossibility?

The barman squinted. Then he realised the truth: the intruder consisted of two superimposed individuals fused into an abhorrent totality, and one was a parasite on the other, but it wasn't feasible to say which was which. Maybe both were parasites on themselves and the vile arrangement was a foul anti-symbiosis. The barman sighed.

"Why don't you try the door?"

"Oh no! My entrance must be *dramatic*. It must always have much of madness and more of sin; and horror the soul of the plot. I am none other than Ford Snapdragon, be aware!"

"Seren-flipping-dipity!" chortled Mr Weggs.

With a sickening plop, akin to the turd of a leprous coprophage hitting a dinner plate, the newcomer sprawled on the floor. Fetid steam rose from his feeble but distended body. He climbed to his feet and clumsily minced over the carpet to the bar, his joints twanging as if his bones were lashed together with chicken wire. He grinned.

The barman winced. The grin was unnatural and unwholesome, partly because the mouth of the fellow was the perfect replica of a sphincter but also because any expression attempted by such a disgusting mutation was bound to be repulsive. Nonetheless he was made of strong stuff and stood his ground like a professional landlord.

157

The mouth puckered obliquely like a torn anus. "Are we all gathered at last? Shall we three beat the meat?"

Mr Weggs said, "There should be four of us."

"Tim Lebbon couldn't make it," answered Samuel Tweed, "but he's not essential to the ritual. Let's waste no more time. If we waste too much, we won't know what we're talking about!"

"Serendipity! I'm with you all the way!"

"Well spoken, Mr Weggs. Follow me, for I'm Samuel Tweed, writer of mystical horror. We must climb the stairs to the room above this one. The ritual can be conducted in privacy there. I hope you have taken good care of your infections? I have taken *very* good care of mine. In fact I deserve an award for the pus. I deserve awards for everything I do, but I never get them. It's unfair! I am Samuel Tweed!"

His soft cheeks wobbled and reddened like blubber jellies in a sunset or like strangely soiled pillows; but no head would ever rest against them, for although attached to his face almost like normal cheeks they gave the impression of having been discarded.

"Follow me!" he repeated.

"No! Follow *me*!" snapped Ford Snapdragon.

"Blimey noumena, I deserve to go first. For the sake of the serendipity of retrocausality! It's my turn!"

"But I am Samuel Tweed! I have a soul and my identity will exist until the end of eternity in spirit form! Atheists don't know what they're talking about! Women don't know what they're talking about! Pacifists don't know what they're talking about! Foreigners from Burma don't know what they're talking about! Mouths don't know what they're talking about! I am the greatest writer of mystical horror! I am Samuel Tweed!"

"Blimey, some very good points, but in the final analysis I am Padgett Weggs and the best of all. Serendipity!"

"No, no! Much of madness, quoth the raven, for I'm Ford Snapdragon! Don't you hear me? I am the best . . ."

"It's reductionist! You don't know what you're—"

158

"The aesthetic noumena of—"

The barman cleared his throat with a menacing politeness and twirled his cudgel casually. The gesture wasn't lost on the three uglies, who with shufflings of their awkward feet managed to convey great timidity despite the scowls on their ludicrous faces.

"It becomes clear to me," said the barman, "that you three individuals are the customers who recently booked a chamber for a private meeting. Until this moment I had assumed my pub was going to host a conference of traders in the confectionary business, for your name, The Gum Chums, led me to that conclusion. I now perceive my mistake. I am Hywel Price, by the way, and I will ask you to control your egos in my presence. By all means have large egos with a solid core; but big fragile *hollow* egos won't be tolerated here. Do you follow?"

Samuel Tweed flared his nostrils and his eyes bulged with pride. "Yes, we are The Gum Chums, true devotees of that wonderful writer, Mr Gum, who passed away from neglect and lack of sunlight several decades ago. We are here to honour his memory and to conduct a ritual that will bring him nearer to us. He's the only writer in history we bow down to, the only author we proclaim as our master."

The barman shrugged. It meant nothing to him what paying customers did upstairs, provided they didn't damage anything. THE TALL STORY had hosted more than one bizarre private meeting in its time, including an odd reunion of bicycle-centaurs, each of which had been winched up the stairs with the aid of a strong nylon cable.

Taking his lack of interest as a dismissal, the trio of freaks hastened to reach the bottom step first. None were capable of moving fast. Samuel Tweed shook like a defrosting trifle, his cheeks pulsing so extremely with each step that Hywel feared they would burst and splash him with face fat; Padgett Weggs shambled and lurched painfully as if impaled on an invisible broomstick; and Ford Snapdragon's joints twanged and juddered like an untuned piano thumbed by a lobotomised baboon.

By letting off a tremendous fart that stank of fermented dandruff, Samuel Tweed was able to increase his velocity just enough to ensure he won this pathetic race. He climbed the stairs in first place; Padgett Weggs came second; Ford Snapdragon was forced to take up the rear, grumbling as he did so, like the same baboon's keeper.

The penultimate wooden step creaked. Samuel gradually lowered himself on his haunches until his oily lips were only a few inches above it and he shrieked, "You don't know what you're talking about!" The impudence of the step had unsettled him; it was thoroughly reductionist. With a twisted leer, he continued to the very top, to a landing. A green door stood before him and he reached out for the knob.

"Blimey, that's the most aesthetic knob I've seen since the noumea was nemonymous!" gasped Padgett Weggs.

"Turn it, for the love of Gum!" cried Ford Snapdragon.

Samuel Tweed nodded in a frenzy.

"I'll do so, the same way the enthralled reader turns the page of one of my brilliant books, for I am Samuel Tweed, the writer of mystical horror. Truly this knob is so fine it deserves an award. So why hasn't it won one? There's cheating going on, I tell you! It's reductionist, that's what it is! My name is Samuel Tweed and I have an eternal soul! Do you doubt me? But I will persist forever in spirit form!"

And he grasped the slimy knob more tightly and twisted it. Silent as a flabbergasted critic, the door swung open. A room was revealed. Bare of furnishings, with a single grimy porthole overlooking a narrow courtyard, it had no character of its own. It was a void. Perfect for the ceremony that was about to take place. Pure nullity.

The only ornament was an ancient short-wave radio that stood on the very edge of a rotten mantelpiece. Some residue of power in its corroded batteries suddenly gave life to the speaker cone as the breeze of the door disturbed it; the faint voice of a meteorologist recited the weather forecast in detached tones, "Light showers may be expected over western parts of the archipelago before midnight . . . "

160

Samuel Tweed strode on chubby tweed-swaddled legs over to the radio and positioned his mouth against the loudspeaker. "You don't know what you're talking about!" he bellowed.

The batteries died; the room was utterly silent.

With a frown that cut his brow like a crease in an accidentally folded maggot, Samuel began exploring the room very slowly, evidently trying to detect a vibe of arcane significance.

Padgett Weggs betrayed his impatience. "Show me the biscuit! I want to gauge how aesthetic and retrocausal it is. Expose your custard cream! The serependity of the blinking noumena gives me the power to compel every pocket to disgorge its contents!"

"Much of madness and more of dunking—"

Samuel waved his arms angrily.

"You don't know what you're talking about! Neither of you do! You're like a pair of foreign teachers! I am Samuel Tweed! I wrote a book with a superbly ironic title, *The Man Who Didn't Collect Awards*, then I wrote a sequel with the same title, then another sequel with the same title, then a third sequel with the same title. Why do housewives win the awards? But I am Samuel Tweed. I have a soul!"

So overwrought did he become during this outburst that a stain rapidly spread over his tweed trousers. Padgett Weggs pointed at it and gibbered in glee; it was plain he wanted to wipe it on his beard or maybe even suck it dry, but he couldn't get down on his knees, he was too stiff. Samuel had little time for such antics; he moved off.

And stopped to stand in the centre of the room.

"This is the spot," he breathed.

Padgett Weggs nodded. "Blimey, it's the most aesthetic spot since the zit of nemonymity went retrocausal!"

"And much of ulcers and more of boils—"

Samuel Tweed gestured imperiously. "Sit there, Mr Weggs; and you sit there, Mr Snapdragon; and I'll sit here. Now we form the three points of an equilateral triangle. In the exact centre of this triangle I will place the biscuit, always at the same distance from all our groins. Symmetry is very essential to the potency of the ritual!"

He reached into his pocket and withdrew the biscuit and lowered it on a tissue to the bare floorboards. Padgett and Ford licked their lips, clapped their hands, wriggled their toes; it was a perfect representation of the face of dead Mr Gum, their literary hero.

"As we know," began Samuel Tweed, "none of us has a drop of sperm in his testicles between us, and indeed there's no more sperm anywhere in the world, for it was all used up thanks to an irresponsible prog rock band who made every male ejaculate beyond repair with *the* supreme orgasmic tune. How then are we to play the biscuit game successfully? Only by sex magick may we achieve our goal."

Padgett and Ford gave the expected response, "How? How? Tell us how before we plop our pants. How?"

Samuel's cheeks wobbled and his ears reddened. "Are your infections in good order? Do they suppurate?"

"Yes they are! Yes they do!"

"Then remove your undewear, for only by beating the meat mystically may we conjure up the spirit of Mr Gum. Yes, my friends, tonight we are going to return him to the mortal realm. Mr Gum will appear again in this very room to give us all advice!"

"Writing advice! Creative writing advice!"

"Beat those putrid cocks, comrades, and spray the holy biscuit! Who needs come when we have pus?"

"Who? Who? Tell us who! Nobody!"

By this time, three pairs of trousers had been yanked off, three pairs of soiled underpants had been discarded, and three deformed cocks swollen to ten times normal size, pulsing with yellow infections and yet still limp, were suddenly exposed. Dim light shining through the porthole reflected on pallid thighs and those awful ochre cocks as puffy hands reached out to grasp them and squeeze hard.

All three of the devotees howled in pain, but they continued to squeeze and work their septic tools. As they did so, the howls pulsed a

162

rhythm that was obscene in a wholly original way; and rapidly those bestial utterances became interspersed with urgent calls of what passed in the foul minds of the uglies for tender human passion.

With twisted leers on faces already distorted since birth, the three meat beaters accelerated the movement of their soft hands; they were locked in synchronous timing. Faster and faster they worked and redder and redder turned their faces while greasy sweat poured down oleaginous foreheads and diseased foreskins were dragged back and forth over tumescent tubes filled with poison under pressure.

Samuel Tweed screwed his face up tighter and emitted a squeal akin to the distress call of a pig trapped in a commode. Then there was a terrific explosion. It was almost instantly echoed by two other explosions. An arc of yellow spunkpus flew up, then another and another, and all came down on the biscuit, deluging the custard cream from three different directions. The ejaculating hacks sagged. All three cocks had burst and hung flaccid like empty horsemeat sausage skins.

Samuel, Padgett and Ford were exhausted; but their efforts hadn't been in vain. The gloopy steam that rose from the mingled pus formed an outline directly over the saturated biscuit. This outline took definite shape. For a moment the groggy celebrants stared blankly at it, unable to fully absorb the incredible truth of the phenomenon. The vapours stabilised, hardened and floated impassively, then the conjured apparition was finished. It was none other than the ghost of Mr Gum!

"It worked! It worked! He's here!" cackled Samuel.

"Semen-dipity!" chortled Padgett.

Ford Snapdragon had nothing to say. All his vitality had drained away and he remained slumped, barely conscious, his sphincter mouth opening for the occasional intake of air like the mono-nostril of a terminal cocaine addict who falls into a coma next to a set of newly-painted white lines on the road he was attempting to cross.

"Why have you summoned me?" hissed Mr Gum, his jowls wobbling and his pearly eyelids fluttering.

Padgett was about to speak, but Samuel blurted out first, "To worship you and learn from you, O wise master! We have brought you back from the underworld, from the other side, from the dark realms of the mystic spirit, to help improve our prose styles."

"From where? For what?" frowned Mr Gum.

"From the land of the dead, to give us writing advice. Not that any of us really need it, especially not me, for I am Samuel Tweed, the writer of the best mystical horror ever, but you are the only author who ever lived whom we respect. We love you and want to suck your mind off. Yes, our sex magick liberated your ghost from Hades. It was worth the sacrifice of our cocks, which are now useless."

"Not that we had much use for them anyway!" giggled Padgett Weggs, but Samuel scowled at the interruption.

The ghost of Mr Gum seemed utterly confused. "From Hades? From a spirit world, you say? But there is no such thing. Reincarnation is the true fate of living beings. When we die we are reincarnated. I died and I was reincarnated. I was no longer Mr Gum; I shouldn't be here, I don't belong in this form. Your meddling has disrupted the cycle. I don't want to return here as Mr Gum. You imbeciles!"

Samuel recoiled and struggled to pull his underpants back on. "You don't mean to tell me that the Christian verison of the Afterlife is wrong? But I have staked all my hopes on my identity existing forever. Don't you know who I am? Don't you know what you're talking about? It's reductionist, I say! Reincarnation can't be real!"

"I'm afraid that it is," snapped Mr Gum.

Padgett Weggs cleared his throat. "Blimey. Am I right in deducing that there's an empty husk walking around right now who should be housing your soul? I bet the blinking retrocausality of his aesthetic serendipity is quite attentuated. Or possibly not!"

"Who the hell are you?" sniffed Mr Gum.

"Why, your grace, I'm Padgett Weggs, author of 500,000 word salads and the dressing to go with them."

"I don't like you. Shut up," said Mr Gum.

164

Samuel Tweed found it hard to control his blubbering lips. There were tears in his bulging eyes as he said, "It's reductionist, it has to be. It can't be true that my talented identity won't endure for eternity. What will I be reborn as? It might be something awful, like a woman or a foreigner! It's more than I can bear! Much more!"

Mr Gum shrugged, his ghost eyes amused.

Samuel jabbed a finger at him. "What were *you* reborn as? What husk did you occupy before we conjured you here with our magickal biscuit game? What body have you come from?"

Mr Gum guffawed. "Haven't you guessed yet? Don't you feel a hollow ache deep down inside yourselves? I was an unusual case, perhaps unique in the annals of the transmigration of souls. I split into three separate parts at the instant of my death and each part occupied a different body. That's correct, fools! I entered you three!"

"No wonder we were such amazing writers; we had a third of Mr Gum inside us!" marvelled Padgett Weggs.

The phantom grinned mirthlessly. "Yes, but with your mystic biscuit ceremony you have succeeded in *expelling your own souls*! I doubt there is any way of returning them. You are the husks! You've sacrificed more than your cocks today, gentlemen."

There was a sordid silence. And then—

"My precious identity! Lost forever!" shrieked Samuel Tweed. With a sudden leap he sprang from the floor and tumbled towards the door; and Padgett Weggs was close behind; and Ford Snapdragon somehow managed to rouse himself enough to follow their example. But Samuel tripped and fell and sprawled on the floor; and Padgett tripped over Samuel; and Ford tripped over Padgett. Mr Gum giggled at this.

When the hacks regained their feet, Ford was in the lead; Padgett was in second place; and Samuel brought up the rear. They clattered down the stairs in that order, with the ersatz spunk-spook floating right behind them. The barman had gone to see what the fuss was about, and he met them at the base of the stairway, the oak cudgel in one hand. As they passed him, he whacked at their scurrying buttocks.

The impact propelled Ford Snapdragon through the door into the street and his joints twanged discordantly as he tumbled into the gutter, where his moronic head was crushed by a passing unicycle. As for Padgett Weggs, the contact of the wood made his beard fall out but he managed to catch most of the hairs and stuff them into his pocket; he would use them later, instead of letters, to write his next word salad. He also passed through the door, out of the pub, into the night.

The barman whipped the buttocks of Samuel Tweed last of all, but the result was unexpected; the red-faced hack froze in place and actually bent over, jutting his hemispheres further out, as if soliciting more blows. The barman took the hint; his fearsome cudgel rose and fell, and Samuel wiggled and moaned as if enjoying the pain.

It was a perverse and deeply disturbing sight. The barman felt disgust welling up inside him. The tweed trousers fell apart, the underpants also, exposing the bare bum cheeks of the humanoid amoeba. As they smarted and reddened, these cheeks began to closely resemble the upper cheeks of Samuel's podgy face. Suddenly the anus of the besieged behind loosed a fart with a rasp that mimicked human speech. "I don't know what I'm talking about!" it declared, with a nasty stink.

The barman lowered his cudgel and nodded. "At last you've made an honest statement!" He raised his foot and booted out of his pub the verbal bum and the excuse for a man attached to the front of it. At this point the ghost of Mr Gum slipped past and followed its sick admirers into the city. Again THE TALL STORY was empty.

The barman shrugged and went upstairs to investigate the damage the trio of cretins had caused. A little later, the front door opened and a man entered the pub, just as the barman was coming down with the desecrated biscuit gripped in the teeth of a pair of tongs. "Stand at the bar and I'll be along to serve you," said the barman.

The stranger looked around and said, "No drinks for me. I'm late. My name's Tim. I'm supposed to be meeting three other writers here. Do you happen to know if they are upstairs?"

The barman narrowed his eyes. "Sorry, Tim. You've just missed them, but they left this gift for you. Look."

And he extended the tongs with the biscuit.

Tim took the custard cream, popped it into his mouth and chewed with an expression of extreme nausea. It took him several attempts to swallow it and keep it down; he retched often.

"Delicious!" he finally said.

I am a Slimy Man

(an example of the poetry of Mr Gum)

I am a slimy man
slimy   slimy
a creepy sneak of the very lowest order
creepy   creepy
more slimy than the things on this list:
snake, toad, old custard tart,
scum on the surface of a stagnant pond,
pus from a boil as big as a fist,
slobber from the muzzle of a hungry hound
slimy   slimy   slimy

More slimy even than tadpole stew,
worm, newt or leaking eye,
my sweat is like oil, my skin is like lard
and I don't find it hard
to slip slide away
anytime anywhere
The slimiest man that ever can be
that's me

I've tried being firm, I've tried being clean
I wash every day and rub myself down
all with an air of finality
but I'm a slimy guy without any way
to get myself dry

without any say in the matter of my slime.
I can slide along bannisters at the speed of sound
For lubricant: my personality
Why can't I just walk down
like everybody else?
slimy   slimy   slimy

I've never had a girlfriend
and that's no surprise
I'm an unctuous jerk with no appeal
but I don't intend to give up —
Hello young lady, would you like a free copy of my
SELF PUBLISHED POETRY COLLECTION?
I can sign it for you, just tell me your name
and telephone number
and favourite position in bed
One day it will work, I'm sure of that
I'll just keep going until I run out of slime,
the slime that is mine,
the endless slime from my bottomless soul
And if I don't run out
you'll be the first to know, my dear!

Despite my slime I put on a face,
I bow with good grace
at all and sundry and follow them around
hiding my leer behind a smile
If you turn I'll be there
all slimy and vile
ready to hand you a free copy of my
SELF PUBLISHED POETRY COLLECTION
I've got hundreds spare
Come back to my house and count them

if you don't believe me
young lady . . .

And if you don't want one of those
maybe I can give you something else
goosebumps for example?

I don't think it's fair
I'm still alone and unloved
just because I resemble the cud
regurgitated by a cow
on its way to the abattoir.
I could be much worse
a rat in a hearse
driving it, not lying in the back,
or a worm cursed
with an even worse car than that
and I do write verse
which makes me a poet
and sensitive and girls like that
or so I've been told
so don't hold back, young lady,
sit on my knee
all free and easy
while my slimy hand works its way
up under your skirt
without you knowing
Look into my bulging eyes, baby,
and repeat after me
SLIMY IS SWEET
And by the way
what did you think of my
SELF PUBLISHED POETRY COLLECTION?

Don't judge me until you've felt me
that's what I say
being sticky and oozy is fun for a day
and I have no choice
I was made like this
I'm a slick mover with a kiss like a hoover
and a way with words
I'm a poet you see,
a songthrush of fuss, a bard of mucus
I'd change if I could
but I can't so I shan't
it's my fate, my destiny
to be always slimy

Come to me girl
a little bit closer than that
and I'll take you on a journey
up my river of slime
all the way to its source
where I'll be waiting for you
with my lips and my tongue
Heart of Darkness, Soul of Slime
I'll lick you and caress you
all night and all day
until you finally cry:
"The horror! The horror!
SELF PUBLISHED POETRY COLLECTION!"

Author's Afterword

THE FIRST EDITION of this novel featured an *Afterword* that satirised certain pundits of the television arts world. As Joel Lane has already pointed out in his *Foreword*, it was a dubious piece in many ways and that's why I've removed it now. For one thing, it was unclear whether it represented the views of myself or those of my character Mr Gum. Even I am unclear on this point! Poor form indeed when an author confuses his true voice with a character's. Mr Gum is *not* me.

Well, not entirely. To create him I took the bad parts of my character, the egotism, narcissism, megalomania, mixed them together, magnified them and gave them independent life. The bad parts of my own character are probably the same as those of everyone else. So Mr Gum isn't based on any particular individual. I daresay there are Creative Writing tutors out there who are thoroughly decent and likeable people. The satire isn't meant to be universal or specific.

It's just satire for its own worthwhile sake!

I have mentioned elsewhere that the four sections of this book satirise four different targets: the first part is a satire on the teaching of creative writing; the second part is a satire on crime fiction; the third is a satire on detective fiction; and the fourth is a satire on satire itself. That last claim is a clever clogs thing to say and isn't true. How can one satirise satire? It isn't feasible. Sounds good though!

Various reviews of the first edition remarked on the obscenity and the unfettered egotism and puerility of the protagonists. So far, so good. But one or two critics felt obliged to make the suggestion that the book should have featured at least one positive female character — to create a contrast with the male dynamic of the tale, to act as a foil to the juvenile excesses of both Mr Gum and Fellatio Nelson.

172

That's missing the point entirely. It's rather like suggesting that Kafka should have introduced Amnesty International into the plot of *The Trial*, so that Josef K. might be given useful legal advice. There is no objective voice anywhere in *Mister Gum*. It's supposed to be a fever dream without remission or pause, a threnody that spurts wholly and remorselessly from the immature human male psyche . . .

Needless to say, the attitudes of Mr Gum *aren't* my conscious attitudes and I can't think of anyone worse to be stuck on a bus with. But this won't stop critics assuming that I have set myself up as a champion of puerility. Mr argument isn't that puerility is *good* but that it has existed for millions of years, and shows no sign of ever going away, so it must be *potent* and therefore worth examining. That's all.

The Librarian by Guiseppe Arcimboldo, 1566.

ND - #0161 - 270225 - C0 - 229/152/10 - PB - 9781907133183 - Gloss Lamination